TRAJECTORY UNKNOWN

Volume I

A fictional story written by Richard A. Whalen

Copyright @2021 by Richard Whalen

All rights reserved. No part of this book may be reproduced in any form or by any electronic or mechanical means, including information storage and retrieval systems, without permission in writing from the publisher, except by reviewers, who may quote brief passages in a review.

This publication contains the opinions and ideas of its author. It is intended to provide helpful and informative material on the subjects addressed in the publication. The author and publisher specifically disclaim all responsibility for any liability, loss or risk, personal or otherwise, which is incurred as a consequence, directly or indirectly, of the use and application of any of the contents of this book.

WORKBOOK PRESS LLC
187 E Warm Springs Rd,
Suite B285, Las Vegas, NV 89119, USA

Website:	https://workbookpress.com/
Hotline:	1-888-818-4856
Email:	admin@workbookpress.com

Ordering Information:
Quantity sales. Special discounts are available on quantity purchases by corporations, associations, and others. For details, contact the publisher at the address above.

ISBN-13:	978-1-956017-60-1 (Paperback Version)
	978-1-956017-59-5 (Digital Version)

REV. DATE: 12.08.2021

Mr. Richard A. Wilden

TRAJECTORY
UNKNOWN

VOLUME I OF THE TRILOGY

TABLE OF CONTENTS

Chapter 1
A NEW DIRECTIVE 07

Chapter 2
PREPARATION 11

Chapter 3
A BEGINNING 14

Chapter 4
THE AWAKENING 17

Chapter 5
YOUR TURN 22

Chapter 6
KNOCK...KNOCK 26

Chapter 7
UP,UP AND AWAY 31

Chapter 8
CAPTAIN RICK 33

Chapter 9
DISCOVERY 38

Chapter 10
AGREEMENT 43

Chapter 11
MR. BEARS MAKE A DISCOVERY 48

Chapter 12
LOVE AT FIRST BITE 51

Chapter 13
A,B,C'S, 1,2,3'S 53

Chapter 14
WHAT'S YOUR NAME 58

Chapter 15
GOING DEEPER 60

Chapter 16
RICK TO THE RESCUE 63

Chapter 17
THE PLAN 69

Chapter 18
THE LINE FORMS 72

Chapter 19 MAKING IT WORK	74
Chapter 20 THE SEED	79
Chapter 21 NO APPOINTMENT NEEDED	82
Chapter 22 UNDERWATER MAYHEM	85
Chapter 23 HOLY HELL	88
Chapter 24 THE LONG JOURNEY	91
Chapter 25 UP, UP AND OMG	93
Chapter 26 TIME TO EAT	97
Chapter 27 TIME TO GO	100
Chapter 28 HELLO AMERICA	101
Chapter 29 MR. PRESIDENT	106
Chapter 30 OH CANADA!	109
Chapter 31 CIRCLES	112
Chapter 32 BACK IN JAPAN	118
Chapter 33 CITIZENS AT LAST	120
Chapter 34 Q AND A	129
Chapter 35 WHAT IS NEXT	137
Chapter 36 BOBBIE'S WORLD	138

Chapter 1
A NEW DIRECTIVE

A virtual meeting is about to get underway.

"Good afternoon everyone. I am Space Force Commander Wallerford. A special acknowledgement to Space Marshall Adagin, Starfleet Commanded Milaker and Planetary Security force General Zunic all in attendance. We are also pleased to have the Space Force Academy Cadets from 1st year to senior year graduate candidates all present. I welcome everyone on this the 161st day of the 181,287 year of the new era."

"Before I get into the new mission, I need to give those new to our programs in attendance a background as to why we are here today. As you already know the new era started when out 17 major countries no longer needed to compete for world resources with the development of the magna flux drive engines that no longer needed carbon base fuels, electric or otherwise mechanical propulsion and we could get anywhere on this planet within minutes, no borders, no government regulations required anymore and all 17 nations agreed to open all boundaries to everyone. With that 1 united planetary community was formed."

"We have explored the near stars within our Galaxy with many missions. As our life support systems have improved with the passing of time we have been able to travel further into our neighboring star clusters exploring new planets, planetoids, moons, asteroids and other space anomalies expanding our knowledge and only heightening out desires to go further into the unknown. With the magna flux drive engines improving each eon our capability to capture lines of magnetic flux and ride them deep into space have improved to their maximum capability. With that we have been to reach many of the nearest star and 1 in particular that I, myself ventured to only took 35 planetary cycles instead of the 222 it originally took at the beginning of our expansion into space. I have also been on 2 other missions to distant star systems making me one of the oldest alive on this planet. However, I don't feel a day over 154."

"Enough of the past, we are here to take an in depth look to the future of our space programs. For the past 11 cycles we have been experimenting with a new dark energy plasma engine which can be engaged at the outer plane of our galactic disc and propel us to speeds 8 times faster than possible with magna flux drive and ion propulsion assist. We might be able to travel faster than what we have already attained, but the results are not fully back as our test ships are still sending back data that now is many planetary cycles from the actual event time. We are also hoping to go even faster that test results currently show with refining design changes. We know mother can control the acceleration and deceleration, turn and make course corrections. In the past we have received information from stars that are beyond the great barriers of space dust and electron distortions that keep up from getting real data on the star systems in the middle of our own galaxy. But some reports indicated habitable planets beyond our view. Our best guess about the unreliable information we have is not good enough to send our population into deep space away from the safety of our dying planet and star system. We need hard facts, feet on the ground so to say before we can have a mass migration."

"Exciting isn't it. We, the planning commission, have all agreed to make an expedition into the unexplored areas of our galaxy……."

A great roar of excitement erupts from the cadets temporarily stopping the commander.

"Our cadets seem to like this decision. Yes, it will include many of you. You were chosen to be cadets by your genetic make-up that has proven over many cycles to promote longer and stable life functions out in space, the weightlessness, the long periods of deep sleep and the ability to regain full functioning upon arrival at your destinations. New worlds to explore, maybe new colonies to start. But let us not get in front of ourselves…. Study, Excel, Graduate and then Explore."

"Let us get back on mission. I have been honored to be selected mission commander. We have begun to construct 2 separate deep space mission ships to map out the remaining ¾ of our galaxy which we have little knowledge of. One of the ships will leave from the over most side of this star system and travel right in a circular direction just about halfway between the center of the galaxy and the outer rim at an optimum to view all the billions of stars and their associated systems curving from the left to the right in a circular pattern so we can observe all the moons, planetoids, asteroids and possible rogue planets that might be able to support life. The other ship will proceed from the under-side moving in the opposite direction mimicking each other and sending back vital information to us through a system of signal booster stations which will be planted at a distance of 8 star systems in width from each other until we have a complete communication system in place for future travel."

"We will be in a deep sleep for up to and over 125 thousand cycles to complete this mission, but that will be but a mere cycle or so to our bodies while in hibernation. During this sleep time the ship will be scanning millions of stars and their related systems getting the most accurate measurement of the age of the stars and their planets that we could have ever dreamed of, their size, direction and their surrounding planets. Be they gas giants, rocky planets, moons or other materials their exact orbits and physical properties will be deeply explored over a period of cycles for each system. But will be measuring thousands at any given moment in time."

"Each starship mission will have 2 crews of 12. Each crew will have a mission commander, pilot, co-pilot, science officer, engineer, communications specialist, doctor, tactical officer and 2 crew members. 5 male and 5 female crew members who have each paired up. There is a special directive that will waken 1 full crew should a viable host world be found at any time during this mission."

"Of course, you know the main requirements, oxygen, water and a breathable atmosphere. The scanning process will never end. It will fully derive all the information possible from each system, star output, age and life expectancy, each planet or moon and inter space debris will be fully scanned for usable minerals, water, geologic make up, weather, temperature ranges, gravity, core density and its magnetic fields. Life too will be assessed. Orbits of all systems will be plotted along with the associated star's movement within galactic influence zones. Radiation anomalies will be identified that could possibly affect the planets and their possible colonization. Each possible world will be assessed on a numeric scale and when a number greater than 65 as calculated by mother, the Mission Commander and Science crew member from one of the teams will be wakened up for a more detailed inspection. If deemed worthwhile, the remaining crew members will be revived, and the mission stopped. The revived team will explore that world for possible colonization. However, if a rating of 75 or higher is ascertained by out mother ship, the entire crew will be awakened."

"Which of you cadets think they would like to join one of these missions?"

The entire space cadet audience stands up and cheers.

"I would have expected nothing else. Briefing adjourned."

Chapter 2
PREPARATION

This morning I woke up and stared at our star with its reddish orange glow. It's hard to believe that we will no longer be able to live here anymore. Our astronomical physic scientists say the star is turning hydrogen and helium into iron at an increasing daily rate of which is causing the start to get larger and redder. The iron atoms are not as compressible as the hydrogen and helium which are 123 times more compressible than iron. Even though I can't see it happening, every planetary circumnavigational cycle it changes enough to be measurable, but they can't say just when life here will become impossible.

So, here I am sitting in my office looking out into the night sky illuminated with millions of lights from windows and magna flux cars flashing by wondering if it is the right thing to do. Leaving our home world with no chance of ever returning. This next cycle will be exciting as we complete the 2 new and most advanced spaceships ever devised. As I understand this, we will be traveling at least 4 cycles until we get to the outer disc edge of the galaxy where the black energy material starts. The large roundish collection cones, one on either side of the ship, will close the slats that allow any materials to pass through when using the standard hydrogen ion drives. The opening which is about a hundred krubits in area will start the collection of the dark material and start to condense it as the circumference of the cone decreases and narrows down on its way to the nozzle. During this process the materials will start to rub against each other within a controlled electronic field where they will heat up to an extremely hot plasma, pass through the nozzle and expand rapidly into the void of space from a controlled hyperbolic shaped chamber giving thrust to the spaceship. It sounds kind of illogical to me, but the scientists say that the number of particles in a krubit multiplied by a distance traveled will give the mass required, but it gets divided by the time to travel that distance. The faster we go, the smaller the time becomes making the time value become extremely small. Thus, the small matter in each cubit times the distance traveled becomes greater and greater as the time to travel becomes so small that the mass collected becomes large enough to be concentrated into a hot plasma. I guess the right way to say it is the area of the intake times the mass of materials collected times the standard distance traveled then divide by the time it takes to travel that standard distance giving an amount of material collected large enough to run the plasma drive engine.

But as we travel closer to the max speed, the resistance of the black material increases against the outer profile of our spaceship almost as if we were re-entering an atmosphere at a high rate of speed as if a meteorite entering the upper atmosphere. This resistance keeps us from reaching max speed. I'm not sure exactly how fast we will eventually go. The science division reports that .6 max speed is a good target to use as a benchmark. To slow down, all we need to do is open the slats and the resistance from the dark materials will slow us down to a speed slow enough so the ship can turn entirely around and start the ion drive to break our speed down so that we can re-enter the galactic plain. Then with magna flux drive, we can enter any solar system and hopefully into any system having a planet with an atmosphere slowing us down to totally avoiding any burn up in an entry maneuver.

I know that once we embark on this mission, all those friends I know will be gone. It has happened to me before when I went on interstellar missions with just the magna flux and ion propulsion systems and it would take so many cycles to reach out destinations. By the time we returned, many generations would have passed. Therefore, I have resolved myself to not be attached to anyone or thing or get emotionally attached. It may seem cold and unsocial, but my heart is out there, somewhere in the stars.

When the time comes, I may be enshrined as a hero, a pathfinder leading civilization out into a distant uncharted space to ensured safety and continuance of our civilization. The scientists say our star has already started to change into a red monster. The timeline they give is that the increased red radiation will kill all life on this planet and within our star system in a few million cycles making life here impossible. What if the scientists are wrong? What if our planet becomes uninhabitable much sooner?

They don't know, do they? So therefore, we must be preparing now for the inevitable events that are to come. Finding a new home world would be the most important thing anyone could possibly do for our civilization. I can just imagine statues of me and my crew being at the center of all new major cities reminding those that followed of our sacrifices. It could take over a quarter of a million planetary cycles for news of a new of a newly discovered world to get back here if we had to go all the way to the other side of our galaxy, our star would have significantly changed and hopefully our civilization is still safe and able to transverse the galaxy to a new home.

But I still have my fears. I fear the coldness of deep space, the loneliness, the darkness, the silence and most of all, the unknown. When we get to the outer edge of the galactic ring, it will get very cold. Atoms will have no energy left making the temperature fall to almost nothing. In previous missions to the galactic ring edge, our spaceships had artificial gravity produced by rotating the living and command areas around a central core where the engines and fuel were stored. It worked great for interstellar missions. But, when we explored the less dense areas where sunlight and solar winds were reduced, temperatures dropped off dramatically and the lubricants froze, metal became brittle and the rings ground their way through, breaking off the metal and separating the crew from the main body of the spaceship. The section with the crews just floated off without the hope of ever being rescued. That is my greatest fear as we will be entering areas of extreme cold. Our space engineers have designed our living and working areas to be located between the two main plasma engine intake ports with the command center underneath the central core and upside down with the floor of the working areas being the exterior hull. The spinning of the spaceship creates the artificial gravity within the entire spaceship so there are no moving external features. I sure hope they know what they are doing, my life will depend on it.

Chapter 3

A BEGINNING

The Journey begins with a large assembly of politicians, generals and family and friends of the crew. It has never taken this long before and I'm getting bored with all the speeches and well wishing. Starfleet Commander Milaker is up on the podium talking and talking. He never seems to run out of words as I and the other crew members wait behind the stage for our introduction. It's getting close, he seems to be wrapping it up. It seems like an hour or more standing here in our space suits holding our helmets under our left arms. Oh, here we go, Starfleet Commander is now announcing the crews.

"Ladies and gentlemen, I now present you with your 24 wonderful and highly talented deep space explorers. Would you please come forward with the Mission Commanded Wallerford's crew of 12 to my left, and the other 12 members of crew 2 to my right. The 5 senior members are in the front row of each group and the remaining 3 junior members and 2 specialists in the back row. Welcome them all as they have pledged their lives to finding us a new home world where our civilization and way of life can be expanded throughout our galaxy."

My thoughts are just let us get on the ship and start the mission…PLEASE.

Wow, this ship is a monster. They have put enough food and supplies in the storage holds to last the 12 of us for many cycles. There are large areas filled with pre-made housing, agricultural tools, machinery and seeds to start us off with a good chance to be a self-sustaining colony when the occasion arises. We are a peace-loving civilization. We haven't had a war since the start of the new era. When magna flux drive became the standard mode of transportation, there were no more immigration points, no more borders, no more importing and taxation. Over the centuries, boundary lines shifted or disappeared as community's melted into one another, people moved from one country to another without visas or permission. Eventually all borders disappeared, sects and indigenous citizens became diverse. Only local infrastructure is needed. Only one government, but separate cities. So now we have no offensive weapons, just small arms for protection against the unknown.

We start off our mission by heading towards the magnetic pole and finding a flux line that directs us towards our star where we will pick up a strong flux line headed in the direction of the outer galactic disc surface and accelerate quickly until we can no longer ride the flux line and the ion propulsion takes over. Now that we are heading away from our star system and on the property trajectory, we can settle into each of our stasis capsules. Everything is automated and pre planned, therefore we are not needed until the computers find a new world worthy of awakening a team. We will be the first team to emerge from stasis. Lucky us.

The stasis chamber is self-augmented once I lay into position. It takes about an hour to fully shut down the body. During this process, my mind plays tricks on me, so I try and think about the science behind it all. Without a positive subject to concentrate on that is kind of hard to do as I know I'll be asleep for many thousands of planetary cycles. My nerves are saying why are you doing this again, but I know why, my people. Lie down, calm down, and then the injection ports are actuated into my circulatory system. One of the miracles of timeless space travel is the ability to stay alive for vast amounts of time in a stasis chamber. The first thing this machine does is to slowly and methodically remove all of the oxygen from the blood and cellular structure within the brain and body. The oxygen inside me is what causes the body to decompose and all the bacteria and viruses found floating around inside my body are eradicated and then the fluids are replaced with a sterile liquid that won't freeze. The body temperature is lowered and then I will pass out into a coma like state. Once the optimal temperature is reached, all the liquid is removed, and the circulatory system emptied. Now I'll just lie there with the tubes still attached and wait and wait and wait.

Once again, I start to thing about the science, my lifelong quest. I guess the greatest invention of all time was the magna flux drive. Professor Flossenhoffer was the one who was able to isolate lines of magnetic flux.

He stated that the magnetic lines were a fabric that permeated throughout space. But being a fabric, the lines could be separated and concentrated into a continuous line from which the opposing directions of force could surround the concentrated flux and suspend whatever was built around it. By the using of opposing directional forces, the one directional line of flux could be bent to whatever direction the spaceship wanted to travel. This eliminated our dependance upon chemical reactions as the method to propel vehicles or whatever type of conveyance we had used in the past. I remember one of my science classes at the academy. A lab experiment that was to use the magnetic flux to suspend a ring of metal in mid-air. Like the klutz I was then, I turned on the flux machine before placing the metal ring in the center. The ring refused to go thru the flux line. I pushed as hard as possible, but the metal ring just could not penetrate. The like directional force created by the concentrated magnetic line became a solid barrier. I pushed so hard, it slipped from my hand and it went flying across the room clanging on the floor in front of the teacher. He was nice about it. He came to my table with the ring, turned off the magnetic flux machine and set the ring in the center. When he turned the machine on, the ring jumped up and was suspended in air like magic. The metal ring floated up with ease and could slide back and forth along the magnetic flux line, but no matter how much force I put on the metal ring, it remained centered in the force field.

Oh, I'm getting cold, and my thoughts are starting to become fuzzy. It is now time to go to sleep.

Chapter 4
THE AWAKENING

Oh, I'm so groggy. My head feels like it is being crushed by a heavy weight. I know the process, I've done this before, and it takes hours to get me revived fully. First, it needs to slowly warm my body to a safe temperature and re-inject my preserved body fluids slowly into the closest veins going directly to my heart. The process is to fill the heart chamber with fluids then start my heart pumping. The problem at hand is the fluid has nowhere to go as most of the vessels have collapsed under my own body weight. Now the fluids are being pushed into the lungs by my heart as quickly as the tubes can get more liquid into me. In the beginning stages of the long-distance space exploration over half of the crew members have been lost as the heart was getting to much back pressure while trying to expand the collapsed vessels. But one group of space medicine doctors came up with an ingenious plan to reduce the back pressure that blew out many a heart wall killing the unfortunate crew member. A fifth chamber was surgically implanted into the heart between the 2 main pumping chambers with a valve going into each chamber that only opens when the pressure in the heart exceeds a safe level. It lets in excess liquid and allows it to flow back into either chamber when the pressure reduces between beats. First the lungs get expanded, then the heart starts to pump to the brain and the awakening process begins in earnest.

When I wake. I must concentrate, really concentrate in moving muscles to assist the fluids into the lower extremities of my body by flexing muscles in my torso and limbs. It is a necessary process that gets the liquids into the smallest capillary veins and allows my body to fully absorb the full amount of liquids.

That was the one process in Space Cadet training I hated the most, but probably the most necessary class of all.

As I lay there flexing for what seems to be half a light cycle, it gave me a chance to reflect on my life and the challenges that I may be facing when I'm fully revived. Silly isn't it, not knowing just what caused the spaceship to awaken the crew, yet, conjuring up different scenarios as to why we are awake.

I hear noised from the adjacent pods. All my crew members which tells me that mother has identified a high probability planet for colonization.

So sore, so hard to get even my leg to lift out of the chamber. But I persist and finally stand with a little wobble here and a misstep there. I look and see my crew getting out of their pods too. All of them are fumbling and stumbling around no better than me.

"Well let's get some liquids and food into our bodies before we start to work" said I.

We each wobbled into the pantry area and grabbed something hot to drink as our bones were still chilled, but we all made it.

To make matters worse than the wobbly legs, was are traveling thru an area of density variation of the black materials causing the spaceship to buffet about. I take a couple of steps and then the vibrations make my legs even more shaky forcing me to grab onto something or get thrown onto the decking. The natural gravitational force made by the spiraling motion of the spaceship creates a centrifugal force keeping up upright. I remember that in the early days of space exploration they used to have the living quarters built on a ring that revolved around the central core creating gravity, but over the years too many failures happened with moving parts. Apparently ambient water atoms would combine with the lubricants and freeze in the extremely low temperatures encountered the further away from the star we got. When the ring froze, it destroyed the sliding ring connection and broke off from the friction of metal on metal. The crews would only have minutes from the failure until the ring would break away from the main body of the spaceship. If lucky, they could get off an emergency broadcast. But finding them is like finding a marble dropped somewhere in the deepest part of the ocean and telling someone on shore to find it.

This buffeting and sudden jerking is reminiscent of trying to navigate my magna flux vehicle during a star flare situation when it would disrupt the magnetic force lines making all carriages using that magnetic flux line waver back and forth. But we don't have a choice here, we must forge our way thru these variations in density until we get into a stable cell. Luckily, this stopped and may not return for a full planet rotation, or even longer, just bad timing.

I was the first one to make it to the forward control area. Looking at the chronometer I strongly shout out.

"We have been asleep for over 33 thousand cycles, I'm sure nobody back home has lasted as long."

A half-hearted chuckle came from each crew member. It wasn't that funny, I guess. Now let's look at what made mother wake us up. It seems a planet with a 77 rating is out there about .4 years off the opposite side. It is in a wide binary system, the 2nd planet from the two stars. This one is odd, a brown dark stars and the other a hot small white and very bright star dancing around each other.

Mother says it has a breathable atmosphere, liquid water and a mass just about that of our home, a molten core and strong magnetic field. This could be a perfect host for our citizens to colonize. We need to take some time to study this one further.

Almost a full planetary rotation elapses into analyzing the data, we find it has some life in the form of algae and small water amoeba that have helped produce the oxygen, but no sighs of larger land animals and no forest or large vegetation areas. It lies in the comfortable habitable zone but has a pronounced elliptical orbit. The planet is old enough and has enough oxygen for a more mature surface. I need to run the data backwards a few planetary cycles to see if there is something else out there that would interfere with the development phases. I have the science officer push back the planetary timeline cycle after cycle and watch the pronounced elliptical orbit the planet takes, certainly, within the parameters for habitable life. Mother has only been watching this system for the past 3 planetary circumnavigational cycles. The older, larger dark star does not have nearly the output as that of the smaller white star. But as long as the white star is visible, the planet gets enough energy. The orbit is asymmetrical as compared to the dancing rotation of the two stars. A brown star and white star are circling each other at an obtuse angle to the planetary plane.

The science officer says "look, look there, I ran the progression backwards 14 full cycles. See the dark star is passing in front of the white star while the planet is traveling in its elliptical orbit and is at its apogee. The habitable zone is collapsing inward as the energy is diminished by the interference of the dark star. The temperature drops from that of a winter over the entire planet to a deep freeze half-way down to max cold so all life forms on the surface perish. I strain my eyes to see just what is happening from my viewing angle on the projection as the smaller white star is in front of a larger dark brown star and the planet can be seen behind both.

The science officer speaks again and says. "That white reflection you now see is ice covering the entire planet and the surface temperature is dropping fast, almost half way to max cold below freezing killing all surface vegetation. We can't live there if once every 44 planetary cycles the planet goes into a deep freeze cycle. The entire planet changes into a snowball for a few light cycles inhibiting whatever growth may have taken place."

"That is a problem we can overcome with proper shelters for that once in 44 cycle event that only last for a few light periods." I ask mother. "Why is the dark star so much bigger than the white star, it seems to be less dense with the smaller white star having more mass? Does that make sense?"

Mother responds with. "The white star has been stealing hydrogen gas from the larger star. Since the brown star is further from the white star than in most robber binary scenarios, I did not see taking of gas from the brown star, but by reviewing my data, it seems it is the uneven rotation of the brown star around the white start only briefly gives the gravitational pull of then white star a short time to pull off gas from the brown star. By my calculations, the white star will reach critical mass within 154 thousand brown star rotations around it and explode."

I tell the crew. "That makes it a no go for us. We can't stay here."

We haven't slowed down too much, and we look at each other nodding in agreement that it is time to resume our search for another home world. Yes, it is time to go back into the pods. But, let us just stay up a little longer and view galaxy from this vantage point for a few days while we accelerate back to ion drive and back into deep space and start all over again, maybe. Anybody that doesn't want to stay and see the collected data can go back into stasis now. Some go, some stay, it is just an excitement causing a rush to a high level and the let down from not finding what we are here to find.

Here I am lying back down in the stasis chamber and the automated process begins. Once more I slip into a self-induced dream state. I wonder if I really do dream while in stasis, I only remember waking at the last moment. Do I really dream, do I forget my dreams, do I opt not to remember, or do I have no dreams at all. I can only hope that everything goes as planned and I awaken thousands of years from now without hitting a rogue planet or asteroid flung far out of the galactic plain by a supernova or some other kind of cosmic calamity.

Chapter 5

YOUR TURN

There are a lot of would-be planets in the habitable zone, but the compatibility numbers just did notadd up to the minimum requirements of this mission. Some planets are too new and haven't developed enough to successfully support life, some too old and the core has solidified or the atmosphere not right or some with not enough water to support large numbers of colonies. Mother knows best and keeps on searching the cosmos.

We travel another forty-five thousand cycles and have gone more than one third past the center of the galaxy to the other side. I estimate we have scanned well into the billions the number of stars, planets and moons since we re-entered stasis. Mother observes a specific planet for a period of a few years. And it looks promising. Crew 2 is awakened and goes through the same painful process of getting restarted.

Warming blood is pumped into the heart where the easy path for the blood to flow is into the lungs, back to the heat and to the brain. But the artery and vein systems are collapsed and that causes the heart to increase pressure strong enough to blow a hole through the outer heart wall and kill somebody during the revival process, that's the reason for the pressure absorbing 5th chamber which allows the valve to open under much higher than normal pressure and expand with blood in between the chambers and towards the lungs to help temporary reduce the pressure while the arteries and veins expand with fresh warm blood.

Crew 2 commander yells to the groggy crew members to get a leg up and on the floor, get yourself moving as it helps the blood get into the muscles and warms up your bones. Eventually they all stand up with the first up crew member helping the next out of the pods.

"Let's get washed up and dressed so we can look at what mother woke us up for" orders the 2nd crew commander.

"A little fresh algae wafer and warm liquids will help get the fuzz out of your heads. I need you thinking well back at the controls." And the commander leads the way. "You first timers, welcome to the rigors of space travel. We have all been through this before and it won't be the last. But it is worth the pain and headaches that come with reconstituting yourselves."

The science officer rushes his meal and dashes to the control panel to see what mother has found.

"It's a 84% match" he shouts as the other crew members enter the control area. "Look, it has an atmosphere and a brilliant blue glow, oxygen.. water.. clouds.. and a large white pearl for a moon.

There is only 1 star and the orbit around the star is mostly circular with little elliptical variance."

They study the findings further. This planet is tilted 13 degrees on its axis, moon only rotated once in its cycle so it is locked facing the planet. "Mother did us right with this one, but she estimates it will take another .3 cycles to reach this possible new colony for us. We still have a lot to do before we get there, exercising our muscles daily may be the top priority." In the 2 cycles prior to mother wakening us up, the spaceship re-entered the galactic disc on a course to intercept this star system. We have been continually slowing down as our intake vents were opened up and plasma is no longer being produced while the friction of black materials created a resistance to slow us down.

Mother is scanning the planet for other information. The solar system is tilted almost 45 degrees from the galactic plane, the planet's tilt on its axis gives a wider temperature variation than our home world that has no tilt, there is a strong magnetic field around the planet meaning a liquid metal core.

The tectonic plates are in motion and there is considerable vulcanism on all sides of the world. The major drawback is it may have too much water in some areas and none in other areas of dry and arid plains with high towering mountain ridges blocking out moisture.

Getting close now, we can see the vegetative areas plainly, and there is a lot of vegetation and even indigenous life forms in the water, on land and in the air. That's a great sign as life is abundant. But, the areas around the equator are too hot for us so we drift up a magnetic line towards the polar area where it is more temperate to our liking. The vegetation is still lush, but not as overpowering along the central portions of the planet. We circle the planet over and over moving further away from the equatorial areas looking for areas that gives us sufficient amounts of fresh water, stable level land areas, comfortable temperatures day and night and abundant food sources.

Mother identifies a large cove along an inland sea with only a small opening to a large ocean far to the other side. Puffy clouds rise and gentle rain falls daily, the waters teem with life and the animal life on and seems to be mainly vegetarian. We set down on a wide-open beach area between the water and vegetative level lying near a river delta. All our date tells us that this could be a perfect place to establish a fully populated colony. Our science officer is getting itchy to get out and gather samples of the vegetation, soils and maybe some life forms to study. But I as the commander remind the away crew that we should go out fully suited with helmets on breathers activated just in case of a virus or microbial infection. Only the extra crew members will carry weapons. The communications specialist will stay on board to monitor our activities and scan for possible dangers. The co-pilot will activate a drone to scan the upcoming land for our exploration.

The rear cargo ramp is opened, and the away crew walks down the ramp with one crew member jumping off the side to take a defensive posture while the rest get out their equipment. When everything is off, the cargo ramp is closed. The away crew hike into the low-lying vegetation with our science offices stopping here and there to take leaf and root samples from a wide range of plants. There is an animal trail that heads towards the forested area, but we see no animals. The science officer tells us it is probably used early in the morning to get to the river for water and we should have nothing to worry about. We keep on the animal trail towards the forested area and stay in communication with the specialist in the ship telling him how wonderful it is out here.

The science officer spots a large beautiful flower about 6 steps off the path. She pushes her way through the taller vegetation to get to it, but as she pushes hard, she slips off of a root and gets her foot entangled in a sharp thorny entanglement that tears the suit open at the ankle and breaks the skin causing some blood to flow. The crew members cut her out and the medical officer tends to her leg.

"The flower just has to wait" says the doctor. "We need to get her back to the ship for further examination for toxins and stitches."

The crew members lift her up and help her hobble her way back down the trail along the path they came. Unknown to the away crew, the smell of the open wound has awakened the forest. Movement to the left, movement to the right and tall grass just opened with a gigantic heavily toothed mouth wide open and grabbing the science officer pulling her deep into the maze of vegetation screaming until no more screams could be heard from her. Everyone drops their loads and starts running back down towards the ship, one member trips and then screams as another beast pounces upon this fallen one. 3 members left at this time. The vegetation is so thick they can't see where the attacks are coming from.

They reach the path they took from the ship to the path.

"We're going to make it" someone shouts, "just RUN." Yet another member is lost. This seems to be a well-orchestrated attack from all sides. A pack of carnivorous animals that has been waiting along this path for supper to walk by. They didn't attack while we were still going out as they probably didn't recognize us as a food source. Just 2 left and we are getting close to the ship.

"Open the cargo hatch" we both yell as we frantically push our way through the last few……….

With the rear cargo hatch open, the scanners show movement, but do not pick up a heat element as the attackers are cold blooded and show no ambient heat source. The exterior cameras do not pick up any life form as the communications specialist watches out for the remaining crew, but, listens to their screams over the communication devices. Identification markers now just show only 2 members left approaching then ship getting closer. What he doesn't see is the footprints in the sand of a 3 toed monster approaching the rear cargo ramp. It is a chameleon that assumes the color of the ground and surrounding vegetation. Only its large black eye can be distinguished. It stops at the end of the ramp as one of its clan members chase down the last away party member making a desperate dash to the cargo ramp. The weight indicator on the ramp tells the communications specialist that someone is on the ramp, so he closes the ramp thinking it is the last of the away party.

Wanting to aid the last remaining away crew member, he rushes back through the middle of the ship where the stasis pods are. Pushes open the door to the cargo area and finds a sand colored monster looking at him. He turns around and slams the cargo door tight. In a panic he goes to then weapons closet and gets a firearm and fumbles to load it while the monster starts banging against the cargo chamber hatchway. The monster keeps banging against the door pushing the frame further inward until it finally breaks against the weight of this beast. The monster enters the stasis walkway and starts its run at him. He points his side arm and fires it at the now totally visible monster hitting it a least 6 times, but it doesn't stop. It leaps upon the communications specialist digging its talons deep into his chest.

They both fall flat onto the floor and both are now dead.

Chapter 6

KNOCK...KNOCK

Oh, it is time to wake again I think as mother has lost her mind. I look around a nobody else is waking up. Why am I the only one up from my crew? I start flexing muscles and rubbing my limbs to stimulate the circulation yet there is no other sound from within the spaceship. Usually all the lights would be on.

I know we are on a planet or moon as there is gravity pulling me towards the floor.

"Mother, why aren't the lights on?" no answer. "Mother, why did you wake me up and why aren't the other crew members awake?" no answer again. Sitting up I stare at the floor, these bones of mine are getting older and more brittle every time I wake up. I can feel them with every move especially as I slip down to the floor, bang my fist against the wall, opening up my closet and get dressed. I stagger a little then I feel some vibration coming from the outside, but I can't seem to make it out. Must be a danger protocol where mother wakens the senior member to make a judgement call. At least they didn't wake everybody else if it wasn't needed. As I gather my strength the vibrations continue and seem to be getting stronger and they are also fairly consistent in timing. This continues for hours during my wakening adjustment period. I finally get myself totally aware, then BOOM goes ship as I get jostled backwards from where I was standing.

"What's this mother, what is happening to this ship?" I make my way to the front of the ship into the command and control center, but I can't see out the translucent windows. There is no visibility. I check all the instruments to make sure they are working, and they are, we are not moving. We are on a planet with about 2/3 the gravity of our home world and there is pressure on the outer hull. Energy levels are very low, very low throughout the ship.

I continue to check out the systems, all seems to be functioning. But, I see that the power levels are so low. I then open the science station and the chronometer reading pops up. Can this be correct,

What? How? Why are we over 56 million cycles into the future? This is impossible, it can't be, it just can't be!

The pounding has stopped for now, I don't know what was making those noises around the hull. I sit back in the command chair and contemplate what is happening and what must I be doing now. There is no protocol for this. I must push my way through these sequences of events. Sitting for some time pondering many thoughts, the most likely is that we are being… What was that flash, a power surge occurred, there was a flash of light. I look at the power storage cell meter and some small amount of power was added. Strange, very strange. Mother indicates that this addition of power has been going on for all this time we were here. Is this some sort of miracle?

I get up and start to walk towards the life pods. Opening the portal to the stasis room, I notice all the pods on the other side, crew 2, are opened with nobody around. Being in the first pod on the crew 1 side I didn't notice them opened, too groggy, I believe. All the other members of my team are still asleep. Do I awaken them now or let them rest until I can get this figured out. Yes, lets figure it out first. I continue making my way back to the cargo hold area, I see far down the corridor that the door is open. It is not supposed to be open. I grab a light to see better as I walk down the walkway to the back end of the stasis room where I stumble upon a pile of bones in the middle of the walkway. An animal with a very large head and sharp teeth, large bones and long tail. Some skin can still be seen between the bones that hasn't rotted away. Under this monster is a communications specialist uniform and his bones. "Oh my, oh my, oh my, what happened here?"

As I walk back to the command center, the booming starts again, over and over every couple of minutes until one seems to be a direct hit as it yanks and pulls on the outer hull. This continues a few more times banging, pushing and releasing. Is one of those monsters like the one who's bones are back in the hallway now outside? All stops again. I sit and wait and wait and wait for it to restart, but it doesn't, not for quite a while. Eventually lighter booming and scraping sensations could be felt along the port side of the ship. This continues for hours and hours. I am afraid that there is another one of those monster like the one in the passageway outside using the ship for a nesting area.

Eventually I fall asleep in the command chair. Don't know how long I've been sleeping for when a ray of light pierces my eyelids. Some of the materials burying the ship are sluffing off and there is light out there. Is there hope that I can safely escape now. I see we are under water now, can I eject in a pod and surface safely?

I don't even know where we are, if the air is breathable, can I survive outside the ship? Let's go back to the historical records and find out what happened to the #2 crew members. After looking and listening to the events for hours, maybe days I came to the solid conclusion that this tragedy could have been prevented.

Crew 2 did not follow strict protocol. I think they were so excited to be on a fresh new planet that they didn't set up a safety perimeter around the ship before starting off. They took everybody except for the communications specialist when they should have left at least 2 members for safety around the ship. They journeyed too far into unknown territory on the first venture and if they properly used the drone. If they properly followed protocol, they might have seen the monsters lurking in ambush. If it were my away team, we would have taken the required precautions and just maybe we would all be alive.

More time passes, a few days or even more as I am not taking count of time and I am still pushing my way through the massive amount of data mother has stored. It appears to be that the 2nd ship found a somewhat suitable home world about 25 thousand cycles out, but, is was located closer into the danger zone in the center of the galaxy, but they stopped there with no more additional information from them. I can't stop thinking we may be the last of our kind. Our star's output was starting to change, which way did it go? How bad did it get? Did we get to another world? Is anybody still alive at our planet? These thoughts consume me these next days.

My stomach growls from the lack of real food. The galley seems to be intact. I look in the food bins and all the food has turned to dust. I open the refrigerator and find nothing inside. I go to the emergency supplies and open one of the prepacked meals. The algae wafers have turned to dust. I wonder if they are still somewhat eatable even though unappetizing. I stick my tongue out and taste the powder. Yuck, horrible, what a mistake that was as I spit out the powder. As hunger takes over my every thought, I remember that the agricultural supplies have specially stored seeds that were made to last forever. Now, I need to find it in the immense storage area. I find the refrigerated storage bin and enter it. Hundreds of encased sealed bags of seeds to be used for a new colony. I need to cut it open carefully as I am now shaking with hunger. Yes, yes, the seeds are still whole. I take a handful and put some in my mouth. They are hear like marbles. Ouch, I think I broke a tooth, so I let them soak in my saliva for a while and hydrate and after a few minutes they seem to be softening up enough to crack open enough to swallow.

I think to myself. How long can I stay in here? I lay down on my bunk crying and chilled and totally alone. I fall asleep for a while, then I am awakened by strange noises around the outer hull. Scraping and banging noises up front. I run to the command center and see the material being sucked off the front vision center thru the translucent material allowing me to see out, but totally protective of anything from the outside. Then something goes swimming by, a large fish, another monster of some kind I presume. This continues, on all sides of the ship it can be felt. It is almost as if the monsters are trying to get into the ship. I need to get this ship to a safe area, this is good I think as the planet has a strong magnetic field and if there is enough power to energize the engines, I could get out of here. I go to the in-line engine and emergency power storage cells, empty! Mother has just stored enough power to keep the living areas intact.

Chapter 7

UP, UP AND AWAY

I hear large scraping noises towards the front of the ship, but I can't see as they are too far back behind the translucent windows in front, sensors are all off-line. Then the same sounds come from the rear. What's going on, what's happening to the ship. A strong jerk from the front, then another and a slight uplifting. Then a jerk in the rear and all goes quiet. I can feel a gentle swaying, we are free, free from the bottom and floating in the water. I can see the surface of the water from the command chair.

The light is getting brighter as the surface approaches. Oh, such a bright light as the top of the ship breaks the surface of the water, blinding light bursting into the command center. Some of these animals crawl over the ship, almost humanoid in nature, but bigger. Then the ship is lifted out of the water, lifted up by these monsters. But, then slowly lowered. It is covered with a protective sheet of some kind. We seem to be moving slowly. Then a thud is felt as it seems to be set on a solid surface.

I can't see thru the sheathing. Yet there is a gentle swaying indicating we must still be on the water.

Some more time pass and it starts to get dark, night time it must be. Curiosity always seems to get the best of me, always has and maybe that's what made me who I am. So, I'll do it, venture out. There isn't enough power to open the rear cargo hatch so what do I do. Remembering the construction of the ship there are some non-mechanized portals that I can open from the inside without power. The side maintenance access portal to the hyper plasma drive may be my best chance as it is in the center of the ship and lower than the other portals. It will be a best try as these accessways are small and I certainly don't have any excess fat on me so I can maneuver in a tight space and shimmy through the passages to get there.

I unlock the portal from inside and it swings open only to expose water below. I hold onto the outer hatch door and wiggle half my body out so I can get a good look as to where I am. I'm not even thinking about whether the air is breathable or my safety, I just want to get out. There is a rope just an arms-length away and it goes back to the surface of this thing we are sitting on. I have to try to move my body out from the ship with my legs still inside and hold onto the portal hatch with 1 hand to reach the rope. Stretching, I grab the rope and pull it toward me, letting go of the portal hatch and both hands on the rope and both feet inside the portal. I pull the rope closer my body, but my feet begin to slip. Oops, my feet slide out and I begin to swing. I can't leave the ship open, so I kick the portal hatch closed with both feet on an inward swing, perfect. The almost perfect fit leaves no indication that the portal is there, but I know where it is so I can re-enter and get the rest of my crew up when the time is right.

I shimmy to a metallic surface. Jump down and look around. The ship is totally shrouded by a sheathing of a strange material. I look up and down the length of the ship and see that it was carefully set upon cribbing to sustain the weight of the craft. Whoever or whatever did this shows a certain ability to care for and maintain this spaceship. That takes some intellect, maybe there can be some contact, but not just yet. It is getting dark again and everything is quiet around the here, it's a good time to explore, but what is the protocol?

It appears that this metallic object that I'm standing on is tied to a larger metallic object and there is a foot way between them. Slipping out from under the strange material I dart to the walkway and get to the other metallic vessel of sorts. There is some exterior lighting not connected to the sun, its bright so I duck as I need to keep out of the bright light. I keep to the edges of a building, stopping to observe the surroundings whenever possible when a door opens. Then a rather large humanoid figure takes a couple of steps out. It stands quite tall with long arms and legs. It is talking on some sort of hand-held device. Funny noises, I can't understand, but apparently its talking to another humanoid no-where around. It starts moving around barking out large noises over and over as if it was calling for a lost mate. Another door opens from another building at the far end and another humanoid comes over to this one and gives him something, they converse and the other one leaves. It just stands there and puts the item to its mouth and drinks from something it is holding. Some time passes and it just stands there.

Then other doors open and other humanoids pass by speaking to the first thing. It talks back and points over there as if telling those things what to do. Maybe it is the commander of this vessel.

The humanoid walks away to another door and calls in. Now is my chance. I run to the hopefully commander's door, pull it open with some effort and slink along the walls until I find a comfortable spot that I can hide from anything that may come my way. I hear the humming of machines starting and running. The commander comes into the room carrying some big black animal. The commander doesn't see me, but the animal does.

Chapter 8

CAPTAIN RICK

Sitting on the fantail of the tug towing my mining barge and related apparatus up into the cold waters of the Bering Sea, I love to look at the prop wash from the tug widen out and the big barge bobbing up and down a few hundred feet behind. A gaggle of seagulls follow close behind the barge screeching at me as if begging for a handout.

You can tell we are getting close to the claim site as the temperature seems to be dropping, not too far from the receding ice sheet, breaking up and melting in the middle of April. The crew of 10 and a cook will probably be loitering on the dock waiting for me to pick some of them up on the Zodiac and bring them back to the barge. I preferred not to fly up, but, ride the tug with my equipment. It gives me time to think about this year and how I am going to attack the new lease I acquired over the winter. We made enough money last year to fund a large core sampling expedition during the winter months from atop the ice cap on a grid in waters from 50 to 150 feet deep. And, to my surprise, the best results came up on a lease directly adjacent to the lease we mined last season.

We are at the lease site and the tug pulls alongside the barge, we drop an anchor and untie the Zodiac. A tug crew member takes it into the harbor to pick up the remaining crew. Well, here is the part I hate the most, welcoming the crew then telling them to get to work. We need to get to the outside corner to the newly acquired lease site, drop the sea anchors and put the barge over the first set up. The 150-foot-long spuds are hoisted up by the 200-ton crane with a 200-foot-long boom and set into position to stabilize the barge.

The Trommel is started, water pumps energized and a bucket picked up on the number 1 line. The bucket is swung into position and dropped into the water for the first bucket of the day. Up it comes with yards of material and dumps it into the Trommel hopper, on a small conveyer to the Trommel itself that revolves around washing the gold free from the sand and mud, then through the sluice boxes to separate and capture hopefully vast amounts of gold over the next 5 months that we will be mining.

Days pass, one after another with the same routine, over and over. Each crew consists of a crane operator, mechanic, Trommel operator and 2 crew members for each shift. The cook will make 2 hot meals each day, mourning and evening and make sandwiches for lunch and midnight meals. The weather can change rapidly, and we listen the weather reports hourly. We can withstand almost all types of weather except for thunderstorms. We need to re-set up about once a week as the 200 feet long boom can make a wide and long swath around the southerly facing edge of the barge. And now that we are into our 7th week of mining, it is weird that a thunderstorm pops up out of nowhere. Boom down, bucket on deck and everybody into the mess hall.

The winds pick up and rumbling of thunder could be heard, but not seen. Then, suddenly a bolt of lightning comes crashing down and hits the water about 50 feet from the barge. I think to myself that was funny. It didn't hit the all metal barge and a 200 feet long crane boom. I remembered that last season a thunderstorm passed over-head and a single bolt of lightning crashed onto the adjacent claim site somewhere close to where we are now. Weird isn't it?

Storm over, let's get back to work. The next morning when I get up, get dressed and walk over to the kitchen and get my usual, a cup of hot chocolate with a buttered bagel. I asked the cook, if my special K was in there and he responded in the affirmative. Walk outside and stand there staring at the operation, dunking my buttered bagel into the hot chocolate. That's one way to take my daily medicine.

I direct the mechanic to have the operator grab the spuds so we can move the barge over a few hundred feet, we need to get it done before the next shift starts.

Move done and breakfast is served, hot buttered rolls and toast, eggs the way you like them, sausage and bacon. A good way to start the morning or for the late crew, settle down and get ready to sleep. I walk over to the crew cleaning out the sluice box. I remind them we need to get this back together before the next crew starts mining. They nod as usual, I really don't have to tell them, but it is just something reassuring to say that they know I know how important their work is. Sluice box back in place, the first bucket of the new set up drops into the water. While pulling it up, the operator signals me to come over. He says something is putting some resistance to the line, he continues operating.

Next bucket, he says, "there it is again, don't you feel it?"

"No, I didn't feel a thing. I'll go over to the sonar and see if there is anything on the bottom." I come back, nothing on sonar. "Do you think the #2 drum is slipping?"

Mining operations continues with the operator still complaining about the increased drag. I shut it down and get the mechanic to pull the housing over drum 2. He does a full check of all gears, bearings, wire rope windings and finds nothing wrong. I think the operator must be getting a little angry as he swings the boom out and down with the bucket hitting the water hard. The operator lifts the boom up and pulls hard on the 1 and 2 lines and then BOOM, the entire barge is yanked towards the bucket almost knocking me off my feet.

"What the HELL was that" I shouted as the operator hops out of the crane and the mechanic picks himself off the deck.

"Something is down there" he yells.

I tell the operator to get back in the saddle and pull in the reigns. Get the bucket up on deck.

Disconnect it and we'll hook up the spare bucket with the light bar and camera to get a good look.

I wake up the operator from the late-night shift.

"What the hell is going on" he asks, "why did you wake me?"

I want to know if he experienced anything different while mining, resistance, drag, pulling out of the normal range. He nodded, he felt something, but seemed to bounce off easily enough and didn't think it out of the ordinary. Now back to the crane and finding out just what the hell we hit.

We get it all hooked up and a line from the underwater camera on the bucket harness to our computer, swing the smaller bucket out to approximately the same spot he was before. Drop the bucket and with camera down 100 feet into the water with lights on. The water is very murky from the previous mining and takes a while to have the tide wash it out so we can see clearly. We look at the screen with anticipation slowly moving the bucket closer to the barge.

Chapter 9
DISCOVERY

As we pull the bucket closer, we hit the bottom of the sluff pile where the face of the dirt has fallen off to the bottom. We know we are so close, and the visibility gets better than 3 feet. I have the operator slowly raise the bucket up the sluff line. Slowly upward bouncing off the side of the excavation.

"There!" I shout.

A small glimmer of a straight white line with some dirt sluffed off below and dirt clinging above almost straight up to the unmined sea floor. It's not a rock formation as it seems to be in a straight line and has a smooth curved under belly, it's not a seagoing ship as it is a least 10 feet below the sea floor, any modern-day ship would be lying on the bottom maybe partially buried by the shifting silt and sand, but not more than 10 feet under the sea floor bed. I start thinking, thinking hard as the operator and mechanic query me about what to do. I put my hands up partly over my face with the palms out as if to ask them to stand down while I think. If this is some ancient artifact from a long-lost civilization, it could be worth millions, but it would have broken under the pressure of the bucket being hung up on it. So, it has to be some sort of metal that is strong and a non-corroded metal to boot.

This is not good, what if this is an alien technology lost for ages under the sea. We cannot let anybody else know about this. If Russia, China, North Korea or any number of bad actors got wind of this they would try and steal it and they wouldn't leave any survivors. If they came up with a submarine at night, they could kill us all and put the alien item on their deck and slip away. I want to stay here and keep mining with the small bucket, see if we can expose the entire length of the object, use the camera and lights to keep from doing any major damage to it while I figure out what to do. I step out of the crane and everybody else on the barge is looking at us.

"Go back to work, everything is OK" I say.

One of the sluice crew members walks over to me and wants me to see the sluice. He points to the upper box and it is full of large pickers, some nuggets of gold over the size of your thumb. Big Gold and lots of it, wow. But that is not the important thing.

What a headache, I need to think. I sit down on one of the steps to the crane and run different thoughts, different outcomes, different everything through my mind. My first objective is to protect the crew. If this is really an alien artifact this place will be swarming with adventure seekers, exploiters and bad actors. Am I thinking too far in advance, no, just trying to make sense out of this, just trying on my brain.

I climb back into the crane cab and tell the operator not to contact anyone, nobody on the outside can know. I asked him if he called anybody and he shakes his head as to answer in the negative, no. That's good, now I need to tell the rest of the crew and get some sort of consensus as to how we are going to keep this under wraps.

"Keep digging around the object, lets expose as much as possible." I tell the operator.

That evening at diner, I make sure everybody is at the table including the tugboat captain and the cook. I stand up and try to explain what we have been doing for the past hours.

"We have discovered some sort of ancient artifact, vary large and possibly technologically advanced beyond our current knowledge. Nobody is to have any contact with anybody outside the barge for safety reasons."

I try and explain how the outside world would try and invade this location just like Sutter's Mill in California back in the 1800's gold rush where Sutter virtually ended up with nothing for his find.

"We need to keep mining around this object so we can see just what it is and then we will set back down again and go over our options."

Everybody agreed and it was back to work with a new invigorated work ethos. I tell them to give me all their phones, cameras and computers, no matter if they can get Wi-Fi or not, just put your names on them and you will get them back. No communications with the outside at all……

I went back to my cabin and put together a work file with the recordings of the underwater find.

Called my daughter back in the lower 48 on the computer portal. She looked at me and asked what was wrong. I had my head down trying to think of the right words to say……a pause.

"We found something, something of great value, something people would be willing to kill over to get."

"Dad, you get millions in gold, people would be willing to kill you over that alone" she said.

Without telling her just exactly what it was, as we really didn't know yet, I sent her over the discovery file for her safe keeping.

"If anything happens to me or our crew, turn this file over to the proper authorities."

"Dad, contact the police or whoever you can trust."

I go to the ship to ship radio and call the U.S. Coast Guard Cutter operating in the Bering Sea. I ask for the captain, he needs to get on the horn. I need to tell him something that will get them over here quickly, but not medical as someone from Nome would come out and that's just what we don't need.

I tell the captain we found a large aircraft, possibly Russian on the sea floor. That got his interest.

They are 120 miles to the southwest and the cutter will be here in 6 hours. Be still my heart, I can't hardly wait. An hour later an Air Force jet starts to circle around our position. You know he is looking for something and he leaves after 5 minutes of circling our position. The entire crew waves to the jet, and watches it head back to the mainland.

The Coast Guard cutter approaches late in the day. I take my lap top computer that has the video of the mining around the craft out of the crane and tell the crew to knock off for the night. The cutter sends over a dory with the captain and 1st mate. They come over to me, I invite them into my office.

They want to know if it is a Russian Badger, a cold war long range bomber that used to operate along the U.S. border. They want to know if it has any atomic weapons aboard. I tell them I have it all on my computer, but hold on, it may not be Russian, or it may not be a Badger. I try and think of a good way to break the news about what we found. I asked them about the laws of salvage. I asked about national security and they responded it could be of prime national security especially if it had weapons of mass destruction aboard, like H-bombs. I scratch my very thinned out top of my head and I try to formulate the right words to say.

"I want to know if I own this before I show you it, if this is anything of value, do I get royalties, if there are any bombs on board do I get a reward. You must understand this has slowed and even stopped my mining operations and that could be costing me millions."

They hummed around and nodded to each other. They agreed to pay fair value for this, they said.

But I pressed on.

"You had the Air Force fly over so I know there is interest, but this find may be so much more than anyone can imagine. I'll need this in writing from then government at the highest levels. This item is not of this era and may not be of this world," I explained. I flipped my computer around and showed them the latest videos. "This bucket is 10 feet wide and we have excavated over 200 feet of wing edge.

It is buried over 10 feet below the sea floor, it probably has been there for over a million years."

Their jaws dropped. The captain stood up and told the 1st mate to stay there and chat some more, he was getting on a secure line with Washington. I told the 1st mate that we could use some help here.

"Get a large suction dredge and frog men out here to suck the rest of the overburden off the ship, plane, or whatever it is. Get another flat barge out so we can lift it out of the water. Our 200-ton crane can lift as much as 300 tons straight up. But the item is still mine, I want to be fair, I want our government to get whatever benefit they can get from it, but I want the patent rights to all technology derived from then craft."

He nodded his head back and forth and I think he got the message. The cutter sent over a couple of armed personnel for security and the 1st mate returned to the cutter. That took a large load off my shoulders, maybe I can get some sleep knowing the navy has this now.

Chapter 10
AGREEMENT

The very next day and Air Force Bison cargo aircraft landed at Nome Airport filled with dredging equipment, a seal team and underwater specialists. They were also started to tow up a couple of barges from Anchorage. They shut down all civilian lines of communication and closed-down the airport for security reasons. They also dispatched a small fleet which included a light cruiser and destroyers from

Pearl Harbor. I was told that 1 destroyer would come up here and the rest would patrol the Aleutian

Islands and the waters between the main land mass and the Russian borders as a precaution.

We have been shut down for 2 days now and the Navy dive teams got their gear together along with a boat to mount the dredges. They agreed to pump the dredging materials into the Trommel so we could at least get whatever gold there is from the clean up around the craft. The first 2 teams of divers were only down for about 2 hours because of the depth being 100 feet or more. When they came up they couldn't stop saying how amazing this was. It was getting larger and larger with every yard of material sucked off. They said it was definitely some type of flying machine, but nothing like they ever dreamed of before. The 2nd shift of divers couldn't wait to get down there. The Navy also brought a small portable decompression chamber with them just in case of a problem.

They did a great job of cleaning off the top of the craft and we could tell a lot more about the shape of the craft. The next job was to clean out under the craft so we could run lines under it and lift it on the barge that was arriving in a few days. The Department of the Navy has sent up a Rear Admiral to be in charge of the operations. We chatted a lot about how we would handle the extraction. I suggested that it be done at night under the cover of darkness as there were eyes in the sky watching us and it would be difficult to see exactly what was taken out at night. Also, that a large tarp should be placed over it like that of a 3-ring circus tent. The Admiral laughed. But agreed to get something out here tomorrow to completely cover the item.

The gold was the largest chunks we ever extracted, and the quantity was at least 5 time higher than that of the adjacent sections. Could this have been due to the craft we found? Is that why lighting was striking directly over this area? Was it the gold or the unknown craft we found? I can only speculate, but I believe there is something to that.

Digging out beneath the alien craft was more difficult than first imagined. Apparently some hardpack or lava flow congealed below the spacecraft anchoring its landing legs so it could not float up to the surface and kept it stabilized in this position for ages until the oceans rose or the continental plate shifted that it was sitting on slowly lowered allowing it to be silted in and eventually covered over with sand, stone and cobble probably from glacier activity on or over the alien ship. Luckily, we are fully supplied for long periods at sea. With no ability to run to the nearest supply store and get parts so we anticipate that we will need everything, so we have an air compressor on deck and impact air hammers in our equipment shed. We don't know if this alien craft is hollow or full of water, will it float if void of water? I get my mechanic and we sit down at the dining room table and start to draw up a plan for lifting the spaceship. What we know is the alien object is over 300 feet long and about 60 feet wide.

There are 4 landing gear locations that support the craft in its present position. We need to design a lifting system that does not damage the alien craft. We have a large variety of spare metal located in the laydown area behind the quarters. We will get 4 chains with lifting eyelets that will hook up to the lifting block of the crane and weld the ends of the chains to 2 separate lifting bars made by cutting one of the spare 120-foot-long 10-inch H beam spuds in half. Then we need to put spacers in between each H beam making a four-sided parallel form. I sent the mechanic to the spare parts lay down area to look for a smaller spacer that will keep the 2 H beams properly separated. He returned saying we had 5 pieces of 2-inch steel piping 60-foot-long each plus some angle irons that could be welded to together.

The 120 feet obtained by welding the 2 pipes together is just what we need, but we will need to stiffen it with the angle irons as the compression might buckle the 2 inch piping. Well, now we know how we can lift the weight of the spacecraft, all we need to do is find something to lift it with. We don't want to damage the exterior hull of the spaceship and putting it on a steel H beam that might do more damage to it when pulled out of the water. We need something soft but strong to wrap around the underbelly of the spaceship. The mechanic says we have a spare belt for the 120-foot-long conveyor in the spare parts container that we use on the tailings conveyor. That gives us just over 240 feet of continuous rubber just like a large rubber band we can slip it around the underside of the spaceship and then hook it up to the steel lifting frame. But we cannot do it with just 1 conveyor belt, we need two. The other conveyor is the feed conveyor that is only 40 feet long which will only give us 80+ feet which isn't enough to even fit around the spaceship. I look at the mechanic with my head tilted down pointing to the drawing of the conveyor belt.

"We have another on the tailings conveyor which we can take off and use." I tell the mechanic.

That will end our full-scale mining operations until we can get the belt back on after we have finished with all the lifting required. We will have to pull out all the pulleys and drive motor to remove the belt from the conveyor frame.

The mechanic tells me that will be one hell of a job to pull the conveyor belt. I nod in agreement, but what other choice do we have? We have 2 spare head pulleys and will have the 2 head pulleys from each end of the conveyor which we can attach to the ends of the lifting frame. Then thread the conveyor belt uncut thru both head pulleys at either end of the lifting bar and then close both ends so it won't slip off giving us two large rubber bands at either end of the lifting frame. All we need to do is hope that the 3-foot-wide conveyor belt is strong enough to hold the weight. This will take all day. I tell the mechanic to take the 50-ton rubber tire service crane, the welder and 2 laborers and get it done.

We will have to eventually disconnect the tailings conveyor from the end of the sluice boxes and let the tailings fall back into the sea. That will mean we may have to re-process the used tailings again, but it will be worth it, I hope. I don't want to stop mining if at all possible.

The Navy divers had to has to use our air hammers to break up the hardpack around the landing skids.

As the divers break up the hardpack in large circles around the landing skids as they don't know exactly where the landing skids end, each leg breaks free with a large hunk of hardpack still attached. But this means the spacecraft is hollow with no water inside as it is floating. Eventually the alien craft floats free and hits the surface. This was done under the cover of darkness so it could not be seen from a satellite. The tarp was placed over it as it floated to the surface. Then we dropped down the lifting bar.

The first conveyor belt was easily placed around the hull just in front of the landing gear, but the lifting bar wasn't long enough to get the rear belt around the tail section of the alien craft. We had to re-position the first conveyor belt to the inside of the landing gear so the rear conveyor could fit around the rear end of the alien craft and pulled into position underneath. We were then able to lift the craft out of the water and the conveyor belts held.

Now what to do with the spaceship. It was 300-foot-long and our crane was only has a 200 feet long boom. I tell the crew to swing it around with the spaceship perpendicular to the boom and try and set it down on in spud lay down area just on the other side of the wash plant. We were only able to set just 1 end of the spacecraft at a time on the deck while the other end was suspended over the end of the barge. I got the 2 Navy divers with the air hammers to remove the remaining hardpack around the landing struts and skids and then repositioned the alien craft and repeated the sane for the rear end landing gear. We cannot lay it down on our deck so it will have to fit onto one of the 2 dumper barges we used to remove the excess tailings until the barge being brought up by the Navy arrives. I measure the exact distance between the 4 landing struts and plot out just how we can set down the alien ship safely. I get the tugboat captain up on deck and go over with him just how we need to position the barge so the alien ship can be placed and secured. He needs to pull an empty dumper barge around to the mining side next to the crane where we will attach 2 10-inch H beam spuds cut in half and weld them to the deck of the dumper barge at a distance equal to the landing skids. We will set the H beam on the flange's edge so the web is parallel to the deck, then cut out the top half of the flange just a little wider than the landing skids and then set the landing skids on the flat side of the web to support the alien craft. Once secured on the beams on the barge deck, we will reposition the barge on the back side of our mining barge so we can continue mining until the Navy gets up the vessel it wants to use to take the spacecraft to a safe storage facility at the San Diego Naval Base. With all that done we can get back to work making money, I hope.

Chapter 11:
MR. BEAR MAKES A DISCOVERY

It's starting to get dark and I want to get some sleep. Time to get the Bear. Just as I am leaving quarters, my daughter calls to ask why there have not been any email reports from the daily operations over the past few days. I tell her I can't talk right now, but soon she will get everything she needs to get up to speed. I tell her I took her advice and things are starting to move quickly.

Now the Bear. I start calling out his name, no response. I know if he doesn't come right away, he will be here in 5 minutes, he just takes a long time to make up his mind. Mind you Bear is not a real bear, just a large black cat who loves to sit on a high spot and watch the sea gulls fly by. He pretends not to notice them, but I'm always afraid he will take a leap at one and end up swimming in the Bering Sea.

The kitchen doors swing open wide and the cook comes over to me with another hot chocolate, I love hot chocolate. I thank him and enter the living area and go over to the TV room. I ask the crew watching if the ball game is still on yet, but it was over a few hours ago. Being this far west puts us so far behind the games in the eastern side of the United States, so I leave the TV room.

There is Mr. Bear waiting outside my door with his tail sticking straight up except for the last inch of so which is bent at a 90-degree angle and points this way and that way when he walks. I bend over and pick him up, he must be eating extra lately as he seems to be getting heavier. Mr. Bear and I have been best buddies for well over 10 years since my daughter found him and 2 other kittens under a neighbor's shed that was just torn down and the mother cat left. My daughter brought them home and started feeding them from kitten formula left over from the other kittens she rescued. I told her she couldn't keep them, and she promised to give them away as soon as they get bigger and can eat solid food. In a short while she came back with 1 kitten and said it wouldn't eat, the other 2 ate well and fell asleep. I took this kitten that didn't have his eyes open yet and he fit entirely within the palm of my hand even being all stretched out. I started to rub his tummy as he was on his back and felt a large lump inside.

That wasn't supposed to be there I thought and began to gently rub his tummy. I rubbed and rubbed it, all night long. Fell asleep with him on my stomach, awoke up around 4 am and thought he was dead. I got up and started to look for a box to put him into and felt really sad that he didn't make it thru the night. But, while moving around, something happened, and he moved. I began rubbing his tummy once again and shortly thereafter he moved his bowls and then urinated on me. He then opened his big black eyes and started to purr. That's my story and we're sticking to it. I won't go anywhere without him.

I brought Mr. Bear in and put him down in front of his food bowl, but he didn't eat. He started to growl and was looking over to the corner behind the sofa bed. Mr. Bear doesn't act like this I thought. I ask him want is bothering him, he just hissed, and now I know something has crawled into the room.

Was it another crab, just like the one that bit him some time before and wouldn't let go? Every now and then we dredge one up off the sea floor and it manages to climb out onto the decking. I need to look around the room for it before he gets bitten again, silly cat. I'm tired, it has been a long day and I need sleep. I stand up and walk around the desk to the area where Mr. Bear was looking.

WHAT! That is not a crab! It is a child-like figure that stands up in front of me in what looks like a uniform. It pounds his chest with its fist and then outstretches its arm forward with the palm open as if a salute. I'm astounded and do the same back just to let him know I understand and mean him no harm.

I then raise my open hand to my forehead in a regular style salute and snap it back to my side and he does the same.

I look at him with amazement, a light green face with cream colored blotches on the cheeks. There are what looks like gills on his neck, but I really can't see, maybe they are just folds in his skin. On top he is wearing what looks like a helmet, one that looks somewhat like a bike racers helmet, but his head is extended to the rear and that protrusion which seems to balance the front protrusion that has his face with the back protrusion. His body is somewhat similar to mine, but the legs are massive as compared with the feet hardly seem to be protruding, something like elephant legs. He is wearing boots, but it doesn't have the forward protrusion like our feet. His arms come down to his waist. I suppose he is sizing me up the same way.

I really don't know what to do so I'll just wing it. I bend down and slowly stretch out my hand as if a handshake and say. "Hello little fellow."

As I get ready to speak again, a shrill noise comes out of this little body's mouth and I tap my ears and shake my head as to say I don't understand. I can see he is not afraid of me, nor I of him. If he is from the spacecraft, of which I have no doubt, this is a major find. I get up and lock my cabin door. I don't want anybody to know just yet until we establish some sort of communication between us.

He starts to make a gesture by lifting his hand to his mouth and pointing to his moving lips. It looks like he is trying to tell me he is hungry. I gesture back by raising both my hands to let him know I understand. I also make a running action with my fingers moving towards the door where I indicated that I will grab something and walk back here with it. I also indicated that he stays there, where I was pointing to the back side of the chair and hide until I get back.

I leave to the kitchen under the cover of darkness where the cook has retired for the night. Make a quick hot chocolate and buttered bagel, grab a bottle of water and a peanut butter and jelly sandwich that was already prepared for the night crew.

Chapter 12

LOVE AT FIRST BITE

I return to my cabin with my hands full of stuff. I put it down the stuff on my desk tabletop where I put out my hand as to indicate he take what he wanted, but he just looks at me not knowing just what to do. I guess it all looks foreign to this traveler. I break off a large chunk of my buttered bagel and dip it into my hot chocolate so it soaks up the liquid and tastes so buttery smooth. I put it into my mouth and eat it making guttural sounds of enjoyment. He looks at me with his hand out as if asking for a piece of my bagel. I break off a piece of it for him and he just stands there, then he points to the hot chocolate where I dipped my bagel. I got the point and dipped it in for him. He takes a bite off the hot soggy end and his face lights up into a bright wide smile. Looks like he never had anything so good before where he comes from. He wolfs that down, maybe too fast, and burps. Points back to the bagel as I take a sip of the hot chocolate. I understand he likes it and wants more so I give him the paper plate with the rest of the bagel and my hot chocolate. That leaves me with the peanut butter and jelly sandwich and water, probably better for me anyway as my diabetes might act up with too much hot chocolate.

I watch him finish up and he indicates he wants more so I give him the rest of my peanut butter and jelly sandwich. The way he is packing the food away I realize it has been a long time since he ate anything of sustenance. It is getting late and I'm getting really tired. I have to take my insulin shot before sleeping so I go into my washroom, close the door and sit on the toilet to take my shot and also to go to the bathroom before going to bed. I open the door and flush the toilet so he can see me operating the toilet and I indicate to him if he needs to evacuate any part of his body he is to use this toilet by sign language. He shrugs his head as if to say not yet. My bed is located at the back end of the cabin. I lay down and try to go to sleep, if only for a few hours. When

I awake 3 hours later, I feel this lump against my back and just guess who is snuggled up against me, not the Bear, but my new found friend. The Bear is sitting at the opposite side of the room next to the door as if waiting for me to let him out. I guess he is mad at me for not paying attention to him. I go to the bathroom, then let out the Bear and go back to sleep.

I can only imagine the trauma this newly found little fellow is going thru. We need to learn how to speak to each other and I need to become his teacher starting tomorrow.

Chapter 13
ABC'S, 1,2,3'S

The next morning brings a knock at the door. I get up and so does my new friend. I point for him to lie back down and cover himself up. It is my wake-up hot chocolate with special K in it and a buttered bagel, my usual morning treat. I thank the cook and walk out onto the barge and see the mining operations starting back up as if nothing has happened except for this large covered alien spaceship on an adjacent barge. This barge that the craft is on is one of my service barges used to get rid of the spoils and the Navy is sending up a larger barge to tow the spaceship away so I can get back to normal operations. More things to think about. I stand outside to eat my bagel knowing that the little fellow can't have the hot chocolate with my special K in it as it may give him the shits. But I still need to finish eating and get him his own bagel and hot chocolate. I sneak back into the kitchen and start to make a buttered bagel and another hot chocolate when the cooks stops to me and asks why I'm getting a 2nd serving. I have diabetes he points out, so I say I slipped, and the bagel fell to the deck, therefore I need hot chocolate and bagel another but without the special K and the cook finishes making it for me.

I return to my cabin and lock up. I give him his breakfast at the desk and tell him we need to get to work establishing a line of communication between us by sign language and by pointing fingers back and forth at each other. He seems to understand. Lucky me, when I got my master's degree, I was asked to become an associate professor, but declined as I was offered another job with twice the salary of an associate professor. That may have been a mistake, but that is another story.

I take out a legal pad and pen, turn it sideways and start a numerical matrix. 1 then a space, 2 a space, 3 a space, 4 a space all the way to 10. Then repeat under the 1st line with 11 thru 20, then under that line with 21 and so forth until the last line being 91 thru 100. He watches me and I am sure he knows what I am doing. I tear that page off and place it in front of him. He looks at it and then returns back to me. Now to get started with the real work. I write a single dot, then and equal sign and then the number 1 and another equal sign and spell out one so it looks like this:

. = 1 = one, then under that

.. = 2 = two

… = 3 = three all the way to 10 and I am also saying these out loud so he can understand. I look at him while pointing to the 1 line and say slowly "o n e" and I repeat opening my mouth and saying slowly trying to get him to speak the number one out loud. Apparently, he is trying as his mouth is moving, but no noise yet. I put my head down to give my brain a chance to reset and I hear air being pushed out of his mouth trying to mimic my sounds. Wa….. wa….. wo….. and eventually won, comes from him, I encourage this by indicating with my hand and finger movements to stretch out the sound and shorten the time until a resounding "one" come from his mouth, I light up with a smile, thumb up and say.

"Great, good work" and give a thumbs up. "Now let's do the 2."

It takes quite some time, but we get thru 10.

Now that we got thru the basics of math, we need to do some multiplication and see if he follows my lead. I tear off that page and let it sit to my right in between us on the top of the desk. I start another sheet of paper from the same pad. I then write:

1 + 1 = 2, then under that

1 + 2 = 3,

1 + 3 = 4,

1 + 4 = 5,

I look at him and I think he gets it. I think he is a man of great intellect by the way he intensely looks at me and at my attempt at teaching him. So, let's start the next group:

2 + 2 = 4

2 + 3 = 5

2 + 4 = 6

2 + 5 = 7

3 + 3 = 6

3 + 4 = 7

3 + 5 = 8

4 + 4 = 8

4 + 5 = 9

I hear an "Uggggh" sound coming from him. He looks at me and shakes his head as if to say no. What, I think, does he mean, I look at him and shrug my shoulders. He points to the pen making a pincer like motion with his fingers. I understand he wants me to hand over the pen. He takes the pen from table after I put it down and goes over the 1st sheet where I wrote out the numerical grid from 1 to 100. He positions the pen between the 8 and the 9 and draws a straight line down the grid to the level in between the 80's and the 90's just below 88 and then makes another line going all the way back to the left margin and puts the pen down. Well, that's interesting. I study that for a few seconds, then bring the sheet with the grid in front of me. I put my left pinky finger on the 1, my left ring finger on the 2, my left middle finger on the 3, my left pointer on the 4, my left thumb on the 5, right thumb on the 6, right pointer on the 7, right middle finger on the 8, my right ring finger on the 9 and finally my right pinky on the 10 and then stare at him.

He takes his left hand out and pulls the sheet away from me. Gives me a solid look and does what I just did. Puts a left finger on the 1, another on the 2, another on the 3 and the next on the 4. Then takes his right hand and covers the 5, and with the second right finger covers the six, then the 7 and finally, the 8. Interesting, our number system is based on 10 which can be easily explained by the number of digits on our hands and toes. He only has 4 fingers on each hand and apparently their number system only goes to eight. It seems that they don't have a 9 or a 10 in their mathematical table.

Alright, let's do another exercise. I write:

0 + 0 = 0

0 + 1 = 1

0 + 2 = 2.

I look at him and he seems confused. He puts his finger over the 0 + 0 = 0. Does that mean that he doesn't use the number 0 with their advanced technology? The ancients didn't have a zero either. The Romans built a vast empire, the aqueduct and other amazing infrastructures without a zero. It wasn't until we adopted the Arabic numbers that the number zero appears, right? Oh, my head is spinning, I need to go out and get some work done which also give my time to think.I tell my new friend vocally and with hand signals that I need to get some work done and I will be back with some more food. If I spend too much time away from my duties, some questions will arise. So, I get dressed in my work clothes, wet gear and boots, safety helmet on and out the door I go. Back to work, the sea is a little choppy and a light rain is falling with grey skies and a good breeze along with that, but it does not stop us from digging and I need to get the concentrated gold ore sorted and counted from last night's shift. Right now, we are cleaning up the remaining area around where the spaceship was located and there is no sign left on the floor bottom of anything being there. Perfect.

I stand fixated watching the operations and it seems strange to have 2 armed guards from the Navy patrolling the deck. Does it make me feel more secure? Or maybe it is the impending doom cloud that comes with a government takeover. Feeling the cool breeze and occasional rain splash upon my face, it seems to be reality setting in. I think about our breakthrough, some sort of communication between us, but is needs to be expanded. Am I the right person for this? It is still hard for me to comprehend a number system that only goes to 8 and has no 0's. That means they can only count to 64, even though it is 88 on their scale, or about 2/3 of our numerical scale for a quick translation and 1.5 times going the other way from theirs to ours. How will this effect trying to explain distance, time and other variables? that we need to tackle. How long is a mile, 5,280 feet, but that is somewhere around 7,800 in their numerical base. Of course, their feet are nowhere the size of ours, so I probably need to go to the metric system. So why doesn't our country go to the metric system like most of the world went to in the 1900's? I know the old computers used the binary system where they reduced all information into a combination of 0's and 1's, on and off, yes and no. Who says it couldn't be 7's and 8's as long as it is consistent, all things need to be relative and uniform. That is how I need to approach this communication and learning curve, steady and consistent. Nothing like having grandchildren.

Chapter 14
WHAT'S YOUR NAME?

I can't keep calling him you, hey there or whatever comes to my mind. He is an alien life form. Maybe I should call him Ali En. That's kind of obvious, maybe Alf for Alien Life Form like the old TV show, the dog like alien from the planet Melmac. I continue working, but thinking of names, Joe, Bob and other common names.

I stop by the dining room for lunch and eat with the crew. When I leave I ask the cook for another hotchocolate and buttered bagel. The cook leers at me and yells.

"You gotta watch your weight."

I reply, "I know," and take them with me back to my cabin.

When I enter the cabin, he is looking at the math sheets and looks at me with a perplexed stare. I guess he has been trying to assimilate these new things too. Lunch has arrived and he eagerly takes them away from me and sits at the desk to eat. As I watch him eat, I think to myself that he seems to be accepting this well, adjusting to the new surroundings. It must be traumatic to him, but he seems to be handling it well.

I pull out a new sheet from the pad and start to writhe the alphabet down. Aa, Bb, Cc and so forth until I reach Zz. I really can't go any further than that can I? He finishes up his meal and hands me the paper plate and paper cup just like a well-behaved child would do. I just turn around a put them into the trash can at the other end of the desk. He quickly and somewhat eagerly comes to the desk standing to my right. I show him books filled with print and tell him you need to learn how to read and write so we can communicate. I start with the Aa sounding it out for him to repeat. He seems to be able to pick up these guttural changes quickly. We slowly work our way down thru the alphabet where somewhere after the Nn when I hear a loud rumbling from his mid-section. I know what that means, and I point to the toilet in the bathroom. He understands, runs over and slams the door shut. After a few minutes he comes out with a big smile on his face and the smell comes along with him. I walk to the bathroom and see he did not flush the toilet. I signal him over and show him how to flush the toilet, reach under the sink for an aerosol can and spray the air to get rid of the smell.

We finished up the alphabet, we got thru the numbers, now we need to give you a name. I turn to him and say Captain Rick pointing to myself, Rick, Rick over and over. He responds with a slurred answer. I point to him and say.

"What's your name, who are you, what do I call you?"

He responds to me with a shrill that is totally not understandable and there is no way I can say that back nor use it in a conversation. I wave my hands as to say no way, we must get a short one syllable name that I can easily get your attention. Bob, Bob sounds good and it won't bring attention. We do not have a Bob on this crew. I point to him and say.

"BOB, you are BOB from hear on." I put my finger on his chest and saying Bob, Bob over and over. I point to myself and say Rick, then back to him and say Bob.

He repeats, pointing to me, "R..i..c..k," and then points to himself and says "B..o..b."

"Well, we now have a Bob on our crew. I say. "All kidding aside, you are not on the crew. I cannot even let you out of here because there are armed naval guards protecting your spaceship. When you can understand better, I will tell you why. You are learning quickly. I suppose you need to be super intelligent in order to on a spaceship traveling thru the stars using a far advanced technology. If you only knew how important that you and your spaceship is and the need to be protected from the greedy, the power mongers and bad acting countries seeking advantages over others."

Chapter 15
GOING DEEPER

Now that you have the basics down, we need to get to the math and science of this world and see if you have the same science as we do. Here is a dot, point A. Another dot, point B and it creates a straight line, if connected. Another point C directly below B gives us a right angle of 90 degrees and a line connecting A to C gives us a triangle. Another point D below A and across from C gives us a square when connected and all sides equal. Extending points B and C out now gives us a rectangle and so forth.

He nods to let me know he understands.

Next is the circle. I draw a line across the middle and label it as d, for diameter. From the center I have another line going to the outside labeled r, for radius. Now I write the symbol Pi and multiply by the d equal the circumference of the circle, c. He points to the Pi sign, so I write 3.14… to indicate its value and he agrees with me. I guess their math is the same as ours, but it is not really 3.14 to him as they do not have all the numbers, but close enough for him to understand.

Now the science. I open my lap top computer and type in solar system bringing up a picture of our solar system. I point to the earth and tell him this is where we are. He understands. I take my finger and make it traverse the orbit of earth all the way around the sun and tell him 1 year, again he understands with a head nod. I point to the earth and spin my finger around it once as if it were turning and say 1 day, he understands. I tell him and write down 365 days equal 1 year, that's like 500 in their counting.

Now I go back to the circle on the paper and tell him that is our planet earth, then write d = 7,930 miles, c = 24,901 miles, r = 3,965 miles. Then I pull up a picture of earth on the computer and point to where we are.

I think we got far enough along for now and I really need to get to work. I pull up the history channel for him to watch while I am away. I point to the door and signal by waving my hands that in no way was he to go outside, stay where he is. I point to him and give him the thumbs up signal, he returns it signaling to me that he will stay put. He also points to his mouth, and I shake my head, I will bring food.

It is bad enough that we have a spaceship sitting on an adjacent barge and a security crew now present, but what would the crew think if they knew we had an actual space being on board. There is no way the world could find out we have an alien aboard. If he were found he would be taken to a research facility and studied like an animal with no dignity, prodded, studied and maybe even sliced up into pieces. I can't seem to get much work done as these thoughts revolve around in my head. Its lunch time now and I sit down with the crew. They are silent and all staring at me when I sit down. Usually it is too noisy to hear someone talking at the other end of the table, but you can hear a pin drop. The only noise is a chair scuffing the floor when a chair is pulled out or moved. This is not good, I think to myself, what can I say or do to make the crew more responsive?

After I finish my lunch, I get the cook to make me a hot chocolate and a buttered bagel, plus a peanut butter sandwich to go. The cook looks at me, and I put my finger to my mouth and to a shushing sound and tilt my head as if to say it's a secret. They all must know something is going on with me, just need to keep is a secret for a little longer, at least until the Navy barge and tug get here from Pearl Harbor.

When I get back to my cabin, Bob is waiting for me and sees that I have brought hot chocolate and a buttered bagel. He jumps up and claps his hands together above is head and gives me the thumbs up signal. Bob eagerly finishes his bagel and somewhat reluctantly eats the peanut butter sandwich. He then pops up out of my chair and walks to the door pointing as if asking to go outside. I shake my head no and give the thumbs down signal, open the window shades a little so Bob can see the armed guards walking the deck and he immediately knows what that means and sits down on the lounge chair in a disgruntled manor.

When I sit back at my desk, I look at the papers we have been working on and to my surprise, there is scribbling all over. At a more detailed glance, I see that he has written in his language next to each number a corresponding symbol and set of symbols. Then, on the alphabet page is another completely different set of symbols, far more than our 26 letters, and he did it with all the other pages we wrote on.

It is like a Rosetta stone lying out a path to his language. But it is a dead language now. There are no other places on earth that have these symbols as they were in ancient Egypt, or are they? Do I really want to get involved with learning his language while I have all these other things to worry about? I believe it will come about in time.

Chapter 16
RICK TO THE RESCUE

I look at my computer and the low battery signal is flashing, Bob let the computer run after he finished watching the show that I left on for him. I told to him the battery is low and I need to charge it back up.

I take the charger cord out of my desk drawer and plug it into the wall socket and the other end into the computer. At that time the symbol changes from the danger, low battery signal to a filling up over and over sequence indicating power is going into the computer. Bob puts his finger on then charging battery signal and taps the symbol with his finger a few times and looks at me with an intriguing stare. Bob points to the spaceship, takes the end of the cord at the computer in his other hand and points to the spaceship again and again pushing the end towards the spaceship.

"I know, I know, I know I say, you need to charge up the spaceship. But you can't do it with a small low voltage charger."

I scratch my balding head, as say think to myself. There is no way I have a charger that will fit that spaceship. I take out a clean sheet of legal sized paper, turn it sideways and draw a straight line down the middle from one end to the other. At the right side I make a small line going up a half inch or so then turning right for a small way and write above it 6-10 volts and point to the computer charging line.

Just to the right of that another line going up an inch or more then turning to the right with 110 volts written above it and pointing to the wall light fixture, then I do almost straight down and inch or more below the mid-line, and back up and down and up and down again. Its alternating current, and I put my right hand out and start shaking it up and down quickly. I think he understands. I do the same with the 220-volt line that we use for the heavy equipment and pumps, alternating current with up and down lines and waving my hand again like with the

110 volt systems. I go to my computer and turn on the clock. It shows hours, minutes and seconds. I point to the second digits and tap my finger on the deck with my right forefinger and point to the second with my left forefinger and start tapping them both in unison.

"1 second, 1 second, 1 second," I repeat so he gets the timing. Then I point to the waves and draw straight lines down from the start to finish of the waves with an arrowed line in between. I write and say 1 second, then below that I write the number 84, point to the number chard at our numerical system at the 60 and then within his numerical box at the 84 and write 60 = 84, wave my hand in a fast shaking movement and say:

"Alternating current."

I look at Bob and he seems confused and he gives me the thumbs down. Maybe they don't use alternating current. I open my desk drawer and take out 2 paper clips and pull a penny from my pocket. I draw the magnetic lines coming out from the north pole of the circle I drew representing the earth, curving around to the south pole at the bottom of the circle and repeat a few times. I think he follows me. Then I stretch out the paper clips and put one on the paper at the top of the circle to the right and one at the bottom of the circle parallel to the one on the top. Between the far ends of the paper clips I draw a squiggly line connecting the two. I pick up the penny and tell Bob that the steel paper clip needs to be copper to work, copper, not steel. Bob nods his head in agreement.

I take the left end of the upper paper clip and move it rapidly up and down over the north pole, put down the paper clip and point with my finger the electric charge flowing to the right to the end and then down the squiggly line at which time I point to the light and tell Bob that is then resistance which produces the light, heat and energy we get from the electric charge and finally back the lower paper clip to the south pole. Bob still looks unexcited. I take a dollar bill from my wallet, roll it up, take my pencil and a piece of tape to which I attach the center of the dollar bill to the pencil. Go into my desk drawer and get a black pen and a yellow magic marker. Mark the top of the circle and the top edge of the dollar bill in black and do the same to the bottoms in yellow. Lay down the dollar bill over the circle so it matches the axis and the poles. I move each of the paper clips so they match the ends of the dollar bill.

I then retrace the movement of the electric charge from the north to the south from the dollar bill, pick

The pencil up and turn it 180 degrees and lay it back down. Then show the current going from the south pole reversing direction back to the north pole. I lift the pencil up over the circle representing the earth and spin between my fingers on both hands over and over. The spinning shows the black end and then the yellow end cutting the magnetic lines coming from the circle. Then put the pencil down and point my finger running along the upper paper clip to the squiggly lines of resistance back the lower paper clip to the circle and back from the bottom to the top over and over.

"Alternating current."

I look at Bob, no he shakes his head with the thumbs down signal.

Then I go from the base line straight up almost to the top and level off without the line dipping up and down as the 600 volt is direct current that we use for the welding machine. Bob smiles and points to the 600-volt line, shakes his head and gives a 2 thumbs up sign. He is excited, really, really excited. I put my hand on his shoulder and take the charger out of the computer and hold it up. We need to get a plug in that fits the ship. I push the cord end towards the ship and then take my hand off his shoulder and make believe it is a receiving end for the charger cord. Bob looks at me and drops his head down as if disappointed. There is no universal charger port for this spaceship. Bob waives his hands and points to the plug end and shakes his head and actually says no as if it wasn't needed.

I sit back in my chair and put both the palms of my hands over my eyes, pressing them hard into my eyes as if trying to see something that wasn't there magically. Well, there is no way I can do this by myself.

What do we need to get this done successfully? We have 500 feet of welding cord, mainly because we may need it for underwater welding, so we can easily reach the spaceship. We need to be able to get it to the spaceship without the armed guards seeing what we are doing, and this will require help from the crew.

I look to Bob, take the charger cord and ask him if he has a port in the ship for the charging cord. I lift up the computer and hold it towards the spaceship and act as if it were the spaceship, take the cord and push it in and out of the port area. I point to the computer port as if it was the spaceship, we need a port or access connection for the electric charge. I take another sheet of paper, draw a barge where we are located and the smaller adjacent barge where the spaceship is. I draw the buildings and the generators and show Bob how a line can be run from the generator behind the quarters to then spaceship. Bob looks at the ceiling and then to the spaceship. He pauses, thinks and moves his head about as if following a route thru the spaceship until he gets to an area where there might be an access for the charge cord. Bob stands up and waves his hands wildly, he knows of a way. He points to the spaceship and makes signs of him taking out something and bringing it back. A portal that can be modified to our generator cords. I look at Bob and give him 2 thumbs up and shake my head in the I understand way.

Bob goes to my desk and draws a figure to one side and points to the picture and says his name, and again, and again. I nod that I understand. He then draws another nine figures and circles them and points to the spaceship. Nine more aliens aboard. Bob then scratches out 5 figures indicating they are no longer aboard leaving just Bob and four other figures. The power must be too low for him to revive them. This has now turned into a rescue mission.

In order to get this done, we need the full crew to get on board this plan. I go to the dining room and ask the cook for a rolling card with a tablecloth over it. He looks at me in a weird questioning way.

I say, "DON'T ASK." I request that the cook make sure all crew members be at the dinner table, no exceptions.

He agrees. As diner time approaches, I watch the crew members going into the dining room. I tell Bob to climb into the lower level of the cart with his helmet on and stay out of sight under the tablecloth so he won't be seen by the guards. I get the cart out with a couple of bumps over the threshold. I stop outside the dining room door, open it and look in. Everybody is there. I bring in the cart over the threshold, walk over to the windows and make sure the blinds are closed and lock the door to the outside and then to the other quarters hallway so nobody can come in or out. I roll the cart into the middle of the open area where everybody can see. I lift up the tablecloth, Bob gets out and I say joyfully.

"Everybody meet BOB."

The entire crew stands up with a roar, wowing, high fiving and yessing out loud. One of the crew members yell out.

"We knew something was going on, but this, WOW!"

I give everybody the sit-down signal by railing my arms and pushing my palms in the downward direction. I begin by thanking the crew for their loud support. But Bob needs your help I explain.

"He needs to get into the spaceship, there are more crew members aboard that need to be saved.

Bob needs to get into the spaceship to get an access port for and electric charging of the spaceships systems. I need both the mechanic and electrician to work together to make a plug-in port that fits the alien spaceship charge port. But in order to do this, I need some of the crew members to distract the guards for enough time to allow Bob to get to the plank walkway and then to the barge and disappear behind the tarp. Then once again when he gets back with the plug-in port from inside the spaceship to my office. In the time between getting Bob in and out of the spaceship, run the remaining cable from the spool in the equipment container and from the generator to the small barge behind the crew quarters in such a manor as not to attract attention from the guards."

They all agree, even the cook.

They kind of split into smaller groups and start making some sort of lame brained schemes to get this done. I break up the loose chatter by shouting out.

"I'm hungry, let's eat, then have a couple of you come to me later tonight with some plans and I'll decide which will be the best way to get this done. Make an extra seat next to me for Bob, he is a full member of this crew now."

Tonight is hamburger and hot dog night, also baked beans and potato salad. Bob looks at the food and doesn't know what to do. All the crew members grab burgers, dogs and buns from the center of the table, splash on relish, mustard, ketchup and other stuff onto each of their plates and then into their mouths. Bob looks perplexed, I guess this meal is nothing like what he is used to eating, is he a vegan?

I suggest to Bob that he try the potato salad and the baked beans as I like mine mixed up together.

Maybe he doesn't know how to use a knife and fork. I take my fork and stab a baked bean, then putting into my mouth and signal Bob to do the same. He tries the beans, then a small piece of potato. Bob shrugs his shoulders as if to say it's alright and takes a few more bites. He looks around the table and then ask for hot chocolate and a buttered bagel. I signal for the cook to make a hot chocolate and buttered bagel. The cook smiles as he realizes all those extra hot chocolates and bagels weren't for me.

With diner done, it's time to smuggle Bob back to my room and settle in for the night. The last couple of days have been strenuous on me and I need a good night's sleep. I have the mechanic bring in a cot and set it up for Bob. He is a big enough man that he can sleep by himself. Even though I am very tired,

I just can't seem to be able to get to sleep. Too much happening and I can't stop thinking about Bob and our plans to rescue the leftover crew members. How can we get this done without the military finding? out about our new visitors. After about an hour of tossing about, Mr. Bear jumps up on my bed and snuggles into me and starts purring. Petting him is relaxing to me and eventually I fall asleep.

Chapter 17

THE PLAN

How can we get this to work? Woke up this morning with a splitting headache. I got this one scenario in my dreams that is hounding me. I need to wake Bob so I can get this out of my head. He's sleeping like a baby so I gently push the end of the fold up bed with my foot, and push again and next time harder until a loud hissing noise comes from him.

"Get up, we need to talk, NOW."

We sit down at the desk, me in my comfortable chair and him in a wooden chair on the side of the desk. I look at Bob, he seems bright and cheery on this bright and sunny morning, so I hit him with.

"Are we alright, are we good?" pointing at Bob and back at me then at me giving us the two thumbs up, then I hold my fists together and give a reverse twisting motion as if breaking something and a two thumbs down motion. He looks at me with sadness shakes his head in a negative way and smiles back with two thumbs up. Ok, I think we are ready for the kicker. I give Bob a serious stare and point to my head as if tapping my brain would really solve this problem. Ok, am I really, really, ready for this? I draw on another sheet of paper a figure and another smaller figure, point to the smaller one and then to Bob, point to the larger figure and them to me and once again give the two thumbs up signal and he affirms back with 2 thumbs up. How do I get this point across without ruining our trust? I again draw 4 more smaller figures next to Bob and circle them, Bob smiles back. I point to the 4 and then to the spaceship. Bob smiles back and shakes his head with a thumbs up. I think he is truly anxious to get this done. I then draw a picture of the generator on the opposite side of the paper and a line from it to the spaceship. I look at Bob and again he smiles and gives a thumbs up. Then I draw a few arrowheads on the line going towards the spaceship and look at Bob. He is smiling and almost leaning over the table in anticipation. I then start filling in the spaceship starting at the bottom where the line enters it and slowly fill it up with blue ink until it is all colored in. Bob jumps up, claps his hands together and gives me a big two thumbs up. He is very happy as far as I can tell, but I am frowning. I put out the palms of my hands out with fingers up trying to slow this party down. He looks back at me and becomes very quiet knowing something is wrong.

I point to the smaller figure and the larger figure and give the two thumbs up signal. Bob agrees. I then point to the smaller figure and then to the 4 figures circled next to his figure and give the two thumbs up signal. He nods his head saying yes with two thumbs up but in a slower fashion as if he is seeing a problem too. I then point to the circled figures tapping it over and over again, then point to my figure and give the two thumbs down signal. Now for the kicker. I point to the five figures of them and then to the spaceship, lift my hands up, side by side and flap them as if a bird flying away from the barge.

He yells, "NO, NO" and jumps up from his chair and walks around, comes back and says "yes".

He realized that when his crew awakens they will not know anything of the efforts and the friendship between us. The other crew members may see me and the situation as a threat to the mission. They won't know that we rescued them from beneath the sea floor. Then my crew and I will be viewed as hostile aliens holding them against their will.

Bob walks around and around in circles shaking his head in a random pattern as if he is processing this too. He sits back down again and is shaking his head up and down slowly and steadily eying the paper.

Bob is understanding our language much better as he is a very fast learner, but still doesn't speak much as he cannot form the words quite right, as of yet. Bob picks up the pen and puts it on his figure and draws a line down below his figure and draws another figure of himself, takes the pen and starts at another figure in the circle of 4 figure and draws a line down next to his lower figure and draws another figure. He then circles the two figures, points to them and them back to my figure, looks at me a gives me a one thumbs up. As I understand this, Bob wants to revive just one crew member, bring him up to speed as to our situation and see how it goes. Sounds like a plan to me. With a grimace of a smile I give the two thumbs up signal to Bob. That means I will have to be onboard the spaceship when then next crew member is revived. That means more activity that might be noticed by the Navy guards. More probability that Bob and his crew will be discovered.

I stand up, look at Bob and tell him it's time to eat. He knows what that means and crawls back into the lower cart level for transportation to then dining room without me having to tell him to do so.

Gratifying isn't it. Like a child that actually listens to his parent.

We get into the dining room and the cook immediately brings Bob a buttered bagel and a hot chocolate. He actually responds back by saying.

"Ok, good, good," and dunks his bagel into the hot chocolate.

There are scrambled eggs, sausage, toast and jam on the table along with hot coffee. Bob ignores them as he gobbles up his breakfast. I take a piece of toast and put some jam on it and place it on his plate, then a spoonful of eggs.

Bob looks at me with a disinterested look, then pick his plate up and walks over to the cook and says.

"Bagel."

After we finish breakfast the mechanic comes over to me and tells me he has a plan, then the electrician, then the operating engineer, and then it seems everybody has a plan including the cook. I tell them.

"One at a time please, one at a time. Come over to my office and I will listen to each plan one at a time."

Chapter 18
THE LINE FORMS

By the time I push Bob back to my office there is already a line forming outside my door. This, unfortunately, is drawing the attention of the guards on deck. The electrician is first in line, so I get him to help me bring in the cart. I close the door behind me, and Bob pops out from the cart. Bob and I sit down at my desk as if Bob is really going to understand all that is being said. The electrician starts off with a plan to distract the guards. He wants to shut the power off to one of the pumps and when the guards change shifts, cut the line so it will ground out on the metal decking when he turns the power back on. That way he can get the guard to move away from the ramp area so he can safely repair the power line. I tell the electrician that it sounds like a good plan, it might just work and show him out.

Next in line is the operating engineer. He operates the big crane with the bucket and says he could accidently drop a full bucket of payload on the deck forcing then guards to move away while the clean up is undergoing. But that is a lot of wet soggy dirt, sand, stones and clay that would have to be shoveled by hand, at least 10 to 15 cubic yards. That would take a lot of time to do the clean-up. High pressure water nozzles spraying all around, most of the crew shoveling materials off the deck. This just might work, but, let me hear more.

Next in line is the cook. The cook tells me he can make a large distraction by starting a fire in the kitchen, a controlled fire with lots of smoke and make the guards and the crew abandon ship while the fire is being put under control. Now that is a lame brained scheme. A fire at sea with the water temperature cold enough to kill you within 20 minutes if you jump into the water. I would prefer to use the Zodiac boat myself. Just another scenario I guess, but that one goes to the back of the list of possibilities.

Last, but not the least, the mechanic, who came after a couple of other lame brained plans that don't even deserve mentioning. He points out to me that the guards are located inside the steel lay down area where we store our spuds during transportation. The mechanic, Jake, says. "The guards don't know that when pulling the spuds for moving the barge, we really don't remove the spuds fully, just lift them up enough to clear the bottom. However, we can tell the guards to clear the area so we can swing the crane over the area and pull the spuds and lay them down. It only takes 5 minutes to pull the spuds, but I can make it last for an hour per spud."

I think to myself that that would be perfect as an hour could give us enough time to run the welding cable, set up a line to the back side of the smaller barge for supplies and get Bob, myself and the electrician aboard the spacecraft. With all the noise Jake could be making rubbing steel on steel, we could hide any noises that might be made charging up the spaceship. I give Jake a pat on the back and walk him out. I look out the door and nobody else is left for me to see today. Turning back to Bob, I look at him with a serious grimace and tell him it is time for us to get back to work on our communications skills. I walk back to my desk and let Bob sit on my chair. I turn the computer on to the social media page and show Bob how to navigate different topics using the keyboard.

"You need to learn as much as you can by yourself."

Bob smiles in an anxious way so I leave.

Chapter 19

MAKING IT WORK

The next morning, with a plausible plan in place, we start by telling the guards that we are pulling the spuds that keep us in place so we can move to the next phase of our mining scheme. I explain we need the entire area between the kitchen and living quarters and the barge with the spaceship to lay down the 120-foot-long metal beam spuds. That we need to be welding and possibly cutting and grinding the steel. For their own safety they would needs to take a position on the far side of the kitchen area.

Meanwhile, the mechanic and laborer unspool the welding cable and stretch it out from the generator behind the living quarters to the far edge of the work barge adjacent to the barge carrying the spaceship. While pulling the spuds, the crane operator is yelling at everybody to get out of the way as the steel spud may swing and rip someone's head off plus a lot of colorful curse words to make his point. I walk over the barge holding the spaceship. Behind me, the mechanic and a laborer carry a large sheet of plywood on its edge dragging it along the deck, but Bob is walking behind it concealing him from anybody's view. Bob carefully walks down the plankway behind the plywood as not wanting to be pushed into the cold water below until we get under the oversized tarp.

I ask Bob where and how do we connect the welding leads to the spaceship. Bob says there is no connection inside, by pushing his fingers of one hand not the palm of the other and giving me a thumbs down. looks around and decides the leg of the landing gear to be the best place for the alligator clamp end of the welding wire to grab the exterior of the spaceship as the rest of the spaceship is rounded and smooth and won't hold the clip in place. The mechanic hands Bob the negative lead.

Bob just looks at it and says "No."

"But we need to have the ground connected" the mechanic contends.

Kind of trying to understand that the spaceship will be absorbing all of the electrical charge, we really don't need to have it grounded, but the mechanic attached the ground to the small barge's steel surface anyway. Apparently, the spaceship was absorbing electricity from then lightning strikes on the water above its position buried in the sea floor for millions of years. Bob does his best to explained to me that the exterior of the spaceship is like a big battery with thousands of rows of storage cells embedded into the outer shell. Even though the spaceship wasn't directly hit by the lightning, the disbursed charge was enough to keep a minimal charge for life support until the next lightning discharge.

I get on my radio and tell the electrician to turn on the welder at the generator, but keep the heat low, low amperage to start. It seems to be working, no sparks, no arcing of the electricity at all. Bob goes to the hatchway that he crawled out of and we help push him up so he can get back into the spaceship. We stand there waiting for something to happen for what seems like an hour, the generator running and pumping juice into the spaceship. Then about 3/4 of the way back just before the propulsion engines, the rear hatchway opens and Bob waves to us from the ramp way which is suspended above the water over the back edge of the barge. I tell the laborer to get some ¼ inch nylon rope. A shackle, pulley and bring it back quickly without being seen. A few minutes the returns with a few hundred feet of rope. We signal to Bob to catch the line. He nods back and says "OK". Tying the pulley to the end for weight, we toss the rope to Bob and it almost hits him, but he ducked out of the way and it falls into the water. We try again and it misses the ramp completely. But, you know, the third time is always charmed. Well, maybe for the Irish it is, but not this time. Finally, we get it to him. Bob hooks up the pulley to the interior of the cargo hold wall. Not knowing how we are going to get into then spaceship, the mechanic says he will get the emergency escape ladder from behind the kitchen where the emergency rafts are stored. He brings the 30-foot-long rope ladder back and hook it to the rope.

Bob struggles, but gets it hooked up. Our brave mechanic says it won't be a problem and grabs ahold of the ladder and starts to climb up when is swings around so he is facing backwards. But he prevails and makes it up to the cargo ramp. He stands up and waves his arm to me to come on up, and I do, slowly and with much effort. He grabs my arm and helps me up the last few steps and onto the cargo hatch deck. The all-purpose deck hand also wants to come up.

I say "No, stay there and wait for further orders, I do not know what else we may need. Just wait."

We look about in awe, not saying a word following Bob back thru the cargo area with compartments filled with futuristic equipment that Bob stops to point out as we pass the storage areas. We come to a firewall and hatch which was broken down and twisted so we needed to shimmy thru the opening. And then we came to a pile of bones lying in the middle of the corridor. Oh my God. It was a raptor with large teeth and talons, but a perfect fully intact skeleton, what a find. I marvel at its shinny white bones untarnished or discolored by time. I reach out to touch it, but chills run up and down my spine and I withdraw my hand.

Fixated on that menacing head we walk into the crew stasis area where Bob shows me the remaining 9 crew member pods. I ask Bob which one he wants to revive, I remind him just 1, pointing the number 1 with my finger. He walks over to a certain pod and points to it saying.

"This one."

Well it seems like Bob has been learning our language as he properly used it here. I shake my head and say "OK" while Bob wipes off the controls over the stasis pods so he can ascertain the condition of the remaining crew members. He walks down past a few pods and stops a one and shakes his head.

Puts his hands on the pod and mutters s few words in his language and looks back at me shaking his head indicating that member did not make it. He takes a few more steps to the last pod and does the same thing. Apparently these 2 members did not make it meant something to Bob, and I understand why Bob is saddened.

"Let's get moving, we are wasting time. Let's get this one out" I say profoundly.

I can hear the metal spud dragging along the barge deck as the first spud has been removed. The operator did a great job as it took over 2 hours to remove the 1st spud which normally takes 5 minutes.

Great job. I hope it takes as long to remove the 2nd of the remaining spuds.

About an hour into the reviving process the pod opens up and Bob is elated to see the eyes of his crew member open. The reviving crew member moves his head around and around and Bob starts speaking in his own language.

He speaks with Bob. "Commander, Commander Wallerford, what are these monsters behind you?

Are they going to hurt us? I am afraid."

Bob responds with. "There are our friends. They are here to help us. Do not be afraid, they will not hurt you or me. They will feed us too."

The talking lasting for quite some time. It sounds like he is saying the same thing over and over, but what do I know, it all sounds the same to me? Bob gently helps his crew member up and turns him sideways pointing to me and my mechanic and talking to him. Bob turns to me and speaks.

"I tell him you my friend, no hurt, help me, save me, save us. Need hot chocolate and bagel, need food for us."

I sent my all-purpose laborer who was waiting outside to the kitchen to get enough for all. "Get more just in case" I urge.

About 15 minutes later he returns with a box full of buttered bagels and hot chocolate. Much more than we need as he didn't know, just following orders. He climbs up into the spaceship narrowly missing dropping the box held in one hand and holding and climbing with the other hand. Kind of silly as we could have just put it in a bucket and hauled it up with a rope. I guess he just wanted to see the insides of the spaceship. Bob takes a bagel and a hot chocolate to the reviving crew member and makes him eat. Even though this is not their staple source of food, he reaches out and grabs the bagel from Bob and eats more.

Everything seems to be going just fine when out of nowhere comes a resounding… BOOM.

Chapter 20

THE SEED

About 40 years' prior a female child was born to a young Chinese couple who lived in a northern mining city in the Inner Mongolia Autonomous Region. When the child was 3 years old, her father was killed in a mining accident which was quite common during that time. Soon thereafter her mother disappeared. She was alone and had to take to begging for food and shelter. It was difficult, but she managed to get by just like a stray dog. Being chased away by many, but helped by a few understanding compassionate people, mostly older grandmothers. When she was 5 she was ragged, in close that did not fit or match, shoes that were worn out and dirty, and she was very scrawny. One day she was making her usual rounds scrounging for food. She snuck into a general store and stole some food from a basket on a low table, unseen by the proprietor. But, at that moment the local district constable entered and saw her take it and run towards the door. He bent down and grabbed her with his arm around her waist as she tried to wiggle by. He went back into the store with her under his arm with her wriggling about, took out a small coin and put it on the counter and took another sweetbread paying for both. Lucky for her it was the right person who understood what she was going through. He took her back to his office and sat her down with what was normally her daily meal, gave her something to drink and asked her about her family and where she was living. By the end of the conversation he knew he must get her into an orphanage, a difficult task in those days when there were so many unwanted children, mostly female in the system. He took her to a special place in Beijing where children were educated and cared for. Quickly her intellect took everybody at the orphanage by surprise. She quickly surpassed all other children her age continued to out-perform all others at the school.

The People's Republic Liberation Army has a special program for children that excel and are constantly inquiring for new recruits. When she became 8 years old, this child's name and accomplishments were forwarded to the People's Republic Liberation Army command center where she was ordered to be picked up and transported to a secret intelligence school. There she was groomed for loyalty and respect for the homeland of China. China has many imbedded families living throughout the world that owe their livelihood to the People's Republic of China. In Taiwan, the Chiu family has been running an orphanage since Formosa split from mainland China but has long ties to the mainland. And with that, they have been smuggling in special children from the Peoples Liberation Army special services and then arranging for their adoption in the normal way as a Taiwanese orphan arranging for them to be placed into a home in the United States.

In San Francisco, the Wu family came over shortly after the end of World War II and began an exclusive import – export business with Mainland China after which they became a wealthy and respected family in the San Francisco area. In the early 1990's the still young child was adopted from the Chiu foundation in Taiwan with papers showing her parents as unknown and orphaned. The Wu family made sure she got into the best schools from which she excelled. She entered USC at the age of 16 and graduated with a degree computer sciences with honors. Then she went on to Massachusetts Institute of Technology to earn a masters and finally a duel doctorate degree in computer sciences and a minor in physics. She was offered many jobs from her senior year at USC to graduation day at MIT, but had targeted the one company and position she has been training for since she was 8 years old. Ms. Wu was hired as a research and development specialist in a major computer company that had a major contract with the U.S. government designing and building advanced computers. She quickly was promoted to project manager and had her own development staff. The United States government hands out hundreds of design proposals to the scientific community each year. When the government published its desire to have designs for advances security filters for the government's nationwide computer centers. She made sure her team was the one that was going to design and win the large contract with the government. She and her staff proposed a point of entry board the scanned all incoming data for viruses and unwanted attachments, identified phishing attempts and acted as the main firewall for all computers. From the many companies that submitted prototypes the government accepted just one, the system that was far superior to all others, hers. As a prototype, the government required that additional functions to be enhanced and the design modified to fit into their mainframes all across the country and at foreign locations worldwide and even into military mainframes everywhere.

The final product was submitted to the government for final testing. Every governmental department including the military was involved with this product. It passed every test thrown at it and was finally adopted to become the only security screening and filtering system accepted by the U.S. government.

Thousands and thousands of these very expensive highly secretive and specialized boards were produced and Ms. Wu was promoted to vice president of the company. From 2005 on all computers were retrofitted with these upgrades and all new computer systems were required to have these filtering boards installed regardless from which computer company manufactured it.

Unknown to anyone other than Ms. Wu and the Chinese intelligence service, a chip was implanted deep into the board, chip J-24. It had no purpose that effected the performance of the board, but screened all incoming data, memos, orders, emails, etc. It scanned for key words that related to military and strategic information and bounced a copy to what appeared to be a military command center in Honolulu. But appearances are deceiving, they were then bounced to the most secret and mostly unknown area in all of China's intelligence community. This center has no other duty than to receive, translate and read all incoming messages. It was designed to have 5 specialists reviewing these messages at any given time. They were not allowed to have any external contact. No phones or I-pads allowed, no personal devices of any kind ae allowed into the intelligence center and mostly, no ability to send messages out. This way nobody or any unknowing hacker or other intelligence agency could trace their existence. Totally removed from the presence of the world, absolutely secret with only a few generals at the top of the People's Liberation Army aware of its existence.

Chapter 21
NO APPOINTMENT NEEDED

President Xi Jinping's office is located within a heavily protected area and only those invited may enter. General Li walks into the building with his rank, insignia and ID tags indicating he has access to all government buildings. He walks straight to President Xi's office and tells the secretary he needs to see the president immediately. The secretary responds that he is in a meeting and cannot be disturbed.

Looking at President Xi's schedule the secretary barks.

"You don't have an appointment, do you?"

General Li grabs his briefcase that is handcuffed to his left wrist and plops it on the desk with the special markings that only mean top secret and most important material inside.

"I need to speak with the president now, right now. You need to interrupt the meeting right now."

The secretary stands up with head low staring at the desk-top and wondering how the interruption of the meeting will affect this job. Slowly lifting the head and walks over to the conference room door, opens it and sticks his head in.

"Excuse me Mr. President, there is a general out here with a most important message for you."

The President excuses himself from the meeting and goes back into his office and General Li enters.

"I have an eyes-only dossier for you, nobody else can know of this but you outside the military. You need to turn off all listing and recording devices including your phone." Barks the general.

The general walks over to a table with an urn and flowers thereon, but behind it is a switch which he turns off. He goes back to standing in front of President Xi's desk and says.

"You will need your key to open this briefcase."

President Xi looks at him strangely and asks "what key? And what department are you from?"

General Li explains to the president that a special department was set up by high command intelligence with a need to know only and over the years maybe new presidents were not informed of the secret ability of our intelligence community to keep it secret above all else.

"Every week our intelligence service comes in with the cleaning crew and scans all offices for hidden listening devices and bugs to guarantee your security and privacy. There is a key attached to the bottom of the second drawer to your right a little more than halfway back."

President Xi reaches down, pulls out the drawer and feels for the key. He finds it with some astonishment. He tries to release it, but can't seem to get it. General Li tells him to use the letter opener at the front of the desk, which he does use and pops the key free.

"Once opened you must act immediately on the information provided herein" comes from the general.

The President opens the brief case and pulls out the report, scans the title and turns to the first page.

General Li explains.

"An open mike transmission was picked up by our standard monitoring station along North Korean border. An offshore mining barge along the northern Alaskan coast had found a Russian bomber that may have nuclear weapons aboard. As you flip the page, we start to receive secret transmissions from the U.S. Coast Guard ship to U.S. Naval intelligence informing them that they verified that an object not from this planet was found buried under the sea floor and may be a spaceship of unknown origin. The

U.S. Navy then sent out men and equipment to help recover the item. The item was pulled up and places on a service barge. The next pages are from our satellite. The first pictures showed nothing as they removed the item at night. The U.S. Navy placed a tarp over it so it could not be seen from space. The next time our satellite passed over it we used ground penetrating radar which shows up on the next photo and a long item, we think 120 meters long and 20 meters wide."

President Xi Jinping, the 2nd most powerful man on earth looks bewildered by all this. He sits back in his chair pondering the impact of it all. General Li interrupts his thought.

"We think there is alien technology that will lead us far into the future ahead of all other powerful countries and can make up the most respected country in the world, but only if we can get it from the Americans."

President Xi looks amazed by this, but still silent.

The general continues with. "The Americans are sending an auxiliary aircraft carrier up from Pearl Harbor to retrieve this item. We must get there before they do and take the spaceship by force.

We have already prepared the latest Sea Serpent class submarine that was launched last year. That's right, you don't know much about this classified sub, but you did question as to why it cost 3 time more than any other sub that we have built."

President Xi shakes head in acknowledgement.

The general continues. "It has 2 nuclear reactors and a duel shaft drive that can reach speeds well over 40 knots underwater. She is the most silent sub anywhere in the world and has a sonar reflecting surface like our stealth aircraft. Streamlined with no conning tower, just a small hump that makes it look like a whale to the passive sonar systems. If you give the order it can be launched 12 hours once it is fully provisioned and manned. But you need to give the order now"

Chapter 22
UNDERWATER MAYHEM

The USS Port Royal, one of the Navy's newest and best manned cruisers is standing 1/2 mile off the mining barge. She has the best trained fighting men in the world and is equipped with all the latest offensive and defensive weaponry known to man. The cruiser can fight off all attacks from on the sea, above the sea and under the sea. She has a crew of 300 plus another 30 special security officers with orders to protect the barge and the secret cargo at all cost.

Unknown to the USS Port Royal, the Sea Serpent class submarine has reached the north coast of Alaska. Her silent running has eluded all the listening devices planted in the Pacific Ocean from Japan all the way through the Aleutian Islands. She slows down silently, close to the bottom in 150 feet of water just behind a small underwater bluff that partially conceals her just over 1 mile from the USS Port Royal.

The mining operations is making a large amount of underwater noise which can be beneficial to the sub, but also detrimental as the sound waves can bounce off the subs hull and be detected by the passive underwater sonar system of the USS Port Royal. The sub wants to get an exact fix on its position so it silently floats to the surface and raises the periscope with its optical range finder to get an exact distance and course from the cruiser, then returns all the way to the bottom and shuts down. A electronic specialist crew mate of the cruiser picks up some movement from the passive sonar and reports it to the duty officer. They look at the screen and both dismiss it as a large whale passing thru the area and then it disappears from the screen. The Chinese submarine's captain has his position as just over 3,000 meters from the cruiser with the mining barge about another 500 meters beyond.

The Chinese People's Liberation Army Navy sub then releases a small underwater manned scooter that skims the bottom of the sea floor skirting away and around the cruiser all the way to the small barge with the spacecraft set upon it. The two-man crew hooks it to the barge about 10 feet below the water line. They secretively climb aboard the barge and to their amazement see a spaceship. They then take pictures from all angles, return to the scooter and ease their way back to the sub.

The sub releases a small tethered communications pod to the surface where it makes a timed electronic blast to a satellite just as it passed above, and it relays it back to the Chinese intelligence high command headquarters.

General Li has been waiting for these pictures and rushes them back to the president.

"Here is the proof you wanted, clear evidence that this is an alien spacecraft, can you now give the order to take the spaceship no matter what it takes?"

President Xi agrees, the order is given, and they have now let the games begin. At the time of the electronic communication blast, the USS Port Royal picked up the encrypted blast and the direction it came from. They identify a Russian fishing trawler just in international waters that has been snooping around since the cruiser entered these waters which is unusual for these waters.

They mistakenly assume the electronic blast came from the Russian fishing trawler and continue them normal duties. The subs commander receives a message from high command to proceed with the plans and get the spaceship at any, and all costs.

From the underwater portal located on the flat surface of the subs long deck, eight underwater specialists emerge, each carrying a single explosive device with 10 kilos of high explosives. They slide down the side of the sub and land on the sea floor. Each one has an advanced underwater rebreather system which requires just a minimal amount of mixed oxygen in a single tank attached to their back.

Most underwater breathing systems require a lot of air and that leads to lots of bubbles which in turn makes noise that can be detected. This rebreather system has a charcoal scrubber and makes very few bubbles making their presence almost undetectable. They walk the entire 3000 meters on the sea floor as they do not want the noise from an underwater scooter from 8 individual sources being detected.

Once reaching the cruiser, 4 men split to the port side and 4 to the starboard side. Each man having a mine with its 10 kilos of high explosives. Each device has a non-metallic suction attaching device that makes no noise on the hull when being attached. Before they can attach the mines, they need to clean off the outside of the hull of barnacles and other organic algae that might keep the mine from sticking.

They make a small scraping noise that is picked up by the underwater listing post on board the cruiser.

Then the suction handle is locked down in place to they firmly secure the devices, it automatically arms itself. The captain of the watch is notified of the scraping noise which has now disappeared. They listen more, but in a precautionary manor he orders the underwater dive team assemble in the ready room.

The 1st mate of the navy's cruiser whose turn it is on the bridge gathers the team and tells them they need to get into the water and check out some suspicious noises detected around the hull. The underwater team hasn't been active for a while and it takes them over an hour to muster up all the equipment, get suited up and test out the breathing apparatus. They get to the deck and lower the ladder to the water and the first underwater team member climbs down and sees the mine planted on the side of the cruiser. But, the mines are armed and waiting for a signal from the sub. About one and a half hours after setting the charges......... BOOM ..... too late.

Chapter 23

HOLY HELL

The spaceship rocks back and forth from the blast. The tarp is blown off the front and partly rests on the rear portion of the spaceship. The operating engineer on the crane is thrown about in his cab as the glass shatters around him.

"Holly Hell, what just happened, the cruiser just blew up" he yells into his radio phone. I respond back with my handheld radio to all crew members including those that were asleep but were thrown out of their beds by the blast. I swing out of the cargo ramp and run up to the armed guards that were visibly shaken by the blast and tell them to get into a Zodiac craft and head back to port and get help, they do just that. Meanwhile, I go to my quarters and find the ship to shore radio system not working. All cell phone and electronic communications were shut down by the government when they first came out to help recover the spaceship. I stop to think, if we get into Big Red, the emergency escape boat, whoever did this will probably sink it to conceal their presence. I tell the crew it will be safer to be in the spacecraft then try to run away in a zodiac boat. I grab my pistol and a few clips full of bullets and the bear, where is the bear, hiding under the bed of course. I grab him too and get back to the spaceship.

The tugboat was on a dumping run and saw the blast from many miles away.

The captain of the tugboat tried to radio the barge, but no response. He is out of range for my walkie talkie hand-held radio, but he still needs to dump and return and that will take a few hours. He gets out his binoculars and scans the horizon. Then, he can make out the crane boom, but no cruiser, just a lot of smoke. He does the next best thing and calls the Coast Guard cutter to report the explosion.

I tell them all of my crew members to:

"Grab food and water, bagels, peanut butter and jelly and bread for sandwiches. Get them to the spaceship and get them aboard. We probably have less than 5 minutes before the barge gets boarded."

I cut loose Big Red and let is drift away from the barge to act as if all the remaining survivors were in it. As I expected, a missile is fired up from the sub which just surfaced, and it goes to the Zodiac which has gone at least a half of a mile from the barge with the armed guards aboard and it was a direct hit. I should have known that was going to happen before I sent them, too late did I think about that happening. The crew brings about 30 cases of water which is hauled into the spacecraft with cargo nets. The cook runs into the freezer and gets out a full box full of bagels and bread and a few gallons of milk. Other crew members get the butter, peanut butter, jelly and chocolate as I requested. I know we are going to have a stand-off, but we need to get all this aboard the spacecraft before anybody knows we are still aboard and not in Big Red.

Everybody gets aboard the spaceship. Bob has assured me that we can get this spaceship flying if we revive the remaining crew members. With all aboard and the crew somewhat settled I give Bob permission to start reviving the remaining crew members. Just then we hear machine guns firing at Big Red, they sink it after around 100 rounds penetrate the fully covered and enclosed lifeboat. Hopefully they will think they got us all. We are now invisible. In all the rush and excitement, we haven't gone over the rules. I explain that they are to touch nothing unless approved beforehand, leave the bones where they lie and we need to get a place where we can go to the bathroom. I ask Bob how do they go to the bathroom with hand signals. Bob laughs and takes me to a small closet where I can barely squeeze into and hands me a weird shapes suction cup attached to a hose going somewhere and tells me in English.

"One size fits all."

He must have picked up that from being on the computer. We had the upgraded satellite program that did not get affected by the communications shut down, just cell phone and cable internet.

I hear scrapping noises along the outside of the hull and then more light enters from the forward command bridge of the spaceship, Bob assures that they can't see in, but we can see out. I cautiously walk up front to the bridge which is located at the bottom of the spaceship in a position that seems to be upside down to me, but I can clearly see men walking around the deck, Chinese military uniforms and they are hooking up the lifting straps to the front and rear areas next to the supports we have the spaceship resting on….. and these bastards are using my crane to do it.

The spaceship starts to shake, then sway as they lift it. The spaceship hits my living quarters on the deck of the barge knocking out part of the wall as they have the crane boomed down too far and the spaceship is bouncing wildly about. They take us to the hull of the submarine just to the rear of the conning tower hump area of the submarine where they secure it with many straps, giftwrapped for Christmas.

I gather the crew and tell them "we are safe for now" in a quiet voice, "relax and we will work our way out of this situation."

Meanwhile the U.S. Navy Intelligence gets news of the cruiser exploding from all places, the Russian trawler that was spying on us from the beginning. The Navy gets the Air Force to send out a recon plane to see what the situation is. They get a report back… no ship, nobody in the water, no spaceship on the barge. No trace of any activity left, but the coast guard cutter still steams to the location just in case.

The citizens of Nome were told this was a restricted area about 15 miles from port. They heard the explosion and saw the smoke, but didn't respond as they were ordered not to do anything since the discovery and recovery operations started.

Chapter 24

THE LONG JOURNEY

The submarine sinks beneath the water to around 250 feet as the Bering Sea is a shallow sea and works its way to the Aleutian Islands and the open waters of the Pacific Ocean. During this time Bob and his revived crew member start reviving the remaining 3 crew members. Bob and I sit down in the command bridge and start talking.

"I need to know things about this spaceship. Can it withstand deep water, how deep? Can it fly again, as we seem to have restored full power to it? How long, how much, when, what, what, what???"

Bob, in his best beginning English and hand signs responds as best as he can. Bob seems to think we can go to 800 feet in depth before we have to start worrying about the spaceship hull integrity. His best guess as the water pressure is not as high here as that on his planet, because the greater gravity of a larger planet is different on his planet and the air pressure above different making this a best guess scenario. We have plenty of air as the ship is more than large enough to handle us all for many days.

The food supply is questionable as there is no real food source left on the spaceship other than what we brought on board. Eventually Bob's other crew member comes forward and breaks the news to Bob, the others have been revived.

That leaves Bob and 5 others plus myself and 13 of my crew members. I instruct the cook to make hot chocolate with what we have left for the new members of Bob's crew, hand out some rations of peanut butter and jelly sandwiches to our crew and try and get some sleep as we have been up for over 36 hours of stress filled anxiety. Bob offers their sleeping quarters to us, but I look into one of the sleepingareas and it is much too small for me to fit. A few of the smaller crew members squeeze into a bed and the others settle down on the spaceship's floor and get as comfortable as possible. Bob offers me the commanders chair as it is the biggest and I accept, sleep is just what I needs for now. I can hear the quiet noises of Bob and his crew members trying to get the spaceship reactivated. I drift off to sleep.

I don't know how long I slept, but it has gotten very dark in the command bridge. I look at Bob, still working on the control panels. I ask him where we are, and he pulls up a holographic display of the earth. He points to a small group of islands in the northwestern section of the Pacific Ocean as is see an area that reminds me of the Kamchatka Peninsula along the Russian border with northern Japan. That looks like it is in the position where Japan now sits, but it has only islands. That map must be from when his spaceship first arrived on our planet. I look at my chronometer and I presume it is around mid-day.

But is dark, very dark. That means we are more than 500 feet below the surface. How much pressure can this hull take? Was it was designed for inward pressure or just to be tight with no pressure outside.

Because of the extra drag from us on the top of the submarine we are only making 30 knots, more or less. That means about 700 miles a day as I extrapolate that from the distance that we have already traveled and the time we have been traveling. Oh man, I slept for over 10 hours. I guess I needed it and I probably would have gotten in Bob's way. Bob comes over to me and said to me.

"We fix most, most good, can fix rest soon."

I question Bob as to how much longer it will take and Bob puts up 1 finger, then 2, then 3.

"No know yet" he responds.

I take it he means hours, but our hours or his. It really doesn't make any difference as long as they get this spaceship working. Keep it up guys, but I am getting worried and antsy. I'm hungry and walk back to the cook and ask for something to eat. He replies that it's all gone. The crew ate everything.

"Oh my god, that means we will probably be out of water soon" I mutter softly.

The cook nods his head in the affirmative. No food and no water and at least 30 hours before we reach the mainland of China.

Chapter 25
UP, UP AND OMG

Hours pass and I can only think of the worst that could happen if we get to China. Tapping my fingers on the command panel doesn't help either. Bob comes over with a big smile and gives me the 2 thumbs up signal.

"All good, 100% OK good" and another 2 thumbs up.

At least we can understand one another and seem to be working for the same end. I ponder ways we can get the sub to surface. I tell Bob we need to make a distraction so the sub commander will think we came lose. Then he will surface and try to stabilize the spaceship. It is getting late and will be dark soon.

I ask Bob "can we move the spaceship from side to side, wiggling it and getting the submarine to change attitude and direction?" Along with a little body language.

He smiles as if he knows what I'm thinking and gives an over accentuated nod yes.

Bob and the pilot of the spaceship get the magna drive powered up. I point with both hands as to move to the right, west as we are now heading mostly south towards China. We move ever so slightly to the west and I signal to move back again, then repeat. Sure enough, our attitude changes as the submarine responds and starts to surface. We know we are rising as some sunlight is now filtering thru to us. I signal Bob to move slightly back and forth as the sub slowly surfaces. We broke the surface and level off, but damn, a hoard of Chinese soldiers comes out on deck fully armed in a defensive posture.

They check the straps over and over and one of the officers goes below deck, probably to report to the captain that they couldn't find anything wrong. We cannot drop the rear cargo door and cut the straps until the soldiers clear the deck while the submarine makes ready to submerge once again. The good news is that we now have Wi-Fi working again. I can see our position being just south of the island of

Hokkaido coming up on the mainland of Japan about 10 or so miles off the coast. The sub stays surfaced as the captain waits for further orders from high command. It has just turned dark.

I turn to Bob and ask him what he has that we can use to cut the straps when the time comes when the soldiers go below deck and we can get out and cut them. He shakes his head in a no fashion.

"What, no light sabers?" I cry out, "no laser guns that can quickly burn thru anything?"

Bob says "no",

"Anything?" I ask.

"No." Bob replies.

"We are screwed."

I ask Bob if he thinks we can shake ourselves out of the straps. He responds with a negative reply.

"How strong is this spaceship?" I ask, "strong enough to lift 100 tons of submarine?"

Bob laughs and shrugs his arms as if in a not knowing way.

"We try, maybe yes, maybe no" he responds.

The sub is approximately 600 feet long and we are just about in the center of it. I tell Bob to turn the spaceship towards the mainland. Maybe we can beach the sub and find some way to cut the straps.

Bob has the pilot power up to 50% and rocks the sub from side to side. Most of the soldiers slide off the wet surface into the ocean, but a few manage to cling on and work their way to the hatch they came out of. The sub tries to resist while we turn the sub to the west directly towards Japan. I google the surrounding area and see we are close to the Misawa Air Force Base. I have an idea, but it's not going to be easy. I'm sure we can be seen on radar by now as the captain of the sub is well-aware of. He desperately tries to back up the submarine and dive, but to no avail, we are winning the battle.

I tell Bob, "let's go for the whole 10 yards." Bob doesn't know what I mean. I tell Bob "full power, 100%, throttle down and let's kick her in the ass."

Bob understands, somewhat, but enough to know what to do. He tells his pilot to push it. We gain speed towards the coast and it seems as if we are rising. We hear creaking noises as the straps tighten and strain. Looking at our position on my lap-top, I point a little to the left as I try and line up the sub with the Misawa Air Force Base, less than 2 miles inland. We are getting close to shore then the bottom of the sub scrapes the sea floor and gives us an upward push. Now we are way above the water, but the sub is halfway out when we hit bottom again and it forces us out of the water and skims back on the surface. A little more and we are totally out of the water. We keep rising and we are free flying with a 600-foot submarine below.

"It's just 2 miles from then shore" I shout, "we can make it."

We can see the lights coming on at the Air Force Base just above the conning tower bump.

The air force base picked us up on radar. They turn the flood lights towards us. I'm sure they think this is a big blimp heading towards the Air Force Base? There is activity at the base as they try and scramble a few jets, but too late, they were not ready for us as we pull the submarine up towards the center of the east west runway. I give Bob the thumb down signal and he relays to the pilot to set us down, with a thud, right in the middle of the runway, but at the far eastern end. I'm sure the sub's captain was shaken up by this. Before anybody can get to the submarine, we drop the hatch and run to the straps holding us to the submarine. We try cutting them with knives as this is all we have. Bob hands us something that looks like a hack saw and it works cutting through the straps like butter, but the base personnel are gathering. It takes a while to cut thru all the straps on just one side, the far side from the control tower.

We get it done just in time before base security arrives to the far end of the runway. We jump back into the spacecraft, raise the cargo hatch and off we go sliding off to the left away from the control tower. They hope they did not see us slip out. All this is going to shock the world. A secret Chinese prototype submarine flying onto a joint Japanese U.S. Air Force base in northern Japan. What could be more earth shattering than that, maybe an alien spaceship? Did they see us? I do not know and do not want to stick around to find out. The crew of mine and Bob's crew are all laughing and cheering as we fly away, but I'm still hungry.

Chapter 26

TIME TO EAT

I sit down with the crew and start talking about finding some food, somewhere we can land and not be seen. One member tells me there is an all-night Dunkin Donuts next to a mall in Seattle. Good enough, we can get bagels for Bob's crew and breakfast sandwiches for our crew. I show Bob where we want to go. He nods OK and gives me an estimated 2 hours to get there. We rise up about 200 feet above the water as not to be seen on radar and easily slide over to our west coast. While we descend upon Seattle of which we can easily see the lights below. The crew member that suggested this foray points out to the area where the mall should be outside the city. We see it as we slow down and hover for a landing. We pull up behind the Dunkin Donuts and take out a couple of light poles in the process.

The rear cargo hatch opens and I along with the cook walk out into the Dunkin Donuts. We have on our distinctive leather flight jackets with then logo of our barge, the Bering Sea Dragon on the back. We go over to the counter at around 5 am. It is just before dawn and I order 2 dozen buttered bagels, 2 dozen hot chocolates, a dozen hot coffees, 5 dozen donuts, and 2 dozen breakfast sandwiches. The cook grabs my arm and says he has to go, go to the bathroom that is and runs off. I throw a couple of 100 dollar bills on the counter and the counter person asks if I want whipped cream on the hot chocolates. I tell him just give me the full can and keep the change. The cook comes out of the bathroom with a big smile, I hand him a few cartons of donuts and a 4 pack container of hot chocolates to bring aboard the spaceship. He must have told the crew as the rest of my men ran out of the spaceship and jostled for a position in line for the bathrooms, the men's and ladies' rooms, it didn't matter as long as it had a toilet. As each crew member came out, I gave each one a carton or box to bring back up to the spaceship. As the last of the crew leaves then bathrooms' area, I decide to take advantage of it myself and as I reached the hallway.... Oh, what a stench, but I still have to go too. I guess the crew didn't want to use Bob's suction cup thing either and held it until we got here.

All aboard, we take off towards the mountains and set down on a clearing atop a mountain, a logging trail and lay down area for an old timbering operation. There is nobody within miles, perfect place to gather our wits. I could not believe how fast the food disappeared and by the time I got back to the ship, over half the stuff was gone and discarded papers were all over the hallway. Too much sugar.

Boston crème donuts, chocolate glazed donuts and no breakfast sandwiches left. I told the crew to clean this place up.

"We are guests onboard. Pick up all the trash and," I get interrupted by.

"There ain't no trash cans in here."

You can't win them all I say to myself, "just pick the stuff up and do your best to wrap it up into a trash ball."

We are good for the next 6 hours. We open the rear hatch for some fresh air and to get rid of the excess paper we spread around the hallway. Bob and his crew complain of light headedness. I believe they are having altitude sickness at a few thousand feet up above sea level. At sea level they were okay, but our atmosphere must be thinner than theirs was. So, we close the hatch and hunker down while

I formulate a plan of action. I take my lap-top computer and switch over to the TV app. Nothing, nothing, nothing. It's now about 8:30 east coast time and I turn on Good Morning America. Just as I was getting ready to switch channels, the host breaks in with an astonishing statement.

"We just got a few hits that a UFO has landed in Seattle. Posted on face book is a homie shot with a cell phone of what appears to be men exiting a craft. Walking into a Dunkin Donuts and back out, then taking off. Is it real, or just some people getting out of a large bus."

"Someone left the gate open" I yelled while laughing, "and all the wild horses left the corral. We've been had."

I continue switching channels for some time, but no other channel has picked up on this. MSNBC, nothing, CNN, nothing. About a half hour or more later I am watching the Fox News channel when a Fox News Alert flashes across the screen.

"UFO sighting confirmed". The news anchor continues with "Seattle police report numerous 1, 2 and 3 car accidents outside the Seattle Mall around 5 am this morning and all drivers reporting seeing what appears to be a spaceship parked in the lot behind the Dunkin Donuts store. We have cell phone movies taken from the drivers, but only an outline can be seen in the darkness. Our correspondent in Seattle went to the Dunkin Donuts shop and interviewed the employees that were then."

The counter person said "We didn't see nothing of a spaceship, just a bunch of guys come in and order the largest order we ever had."

The correspondent asked, "what did they order."

Employee replying, "5 dozen donuts, 2 dozen buttered bagels, 3 dozed breakfast sandwiches and 4 dozen coffees and hot chocolates…. and they tipped really good."

The correspondent continues with "Did you notice anything else?"

"Yeah," he says, "they all wore the same jacket which said Bering Sea Dragon on inscribed on each of them."

"There you have it" the correspondent finishes up with "proof that America runs on Dunkin."

Well, the cat is definitely out of the bag. And that reminds me that Mr. Bear is still in the makeshift cage Bob make in the cargo hold. I go back and find him, he looks at me and tells me he wants to get out by saying "me out" with a silent t. I look at him and tell him we will get you out soon and give him some fresh water.

"They didn't have cat food at the Dunkin Donuts and you need to go on a diet too." I told him. Really,

I know he didn't understand, but the sound of my voice comforted him.

Chapter 27

TIME TO GO

I gather the crew and tell them. "We are back on American soil now, we have been through a lot and I'm damn sure we won't be able to mine anymore this year as the Navy will probably be taking over the site recovering pieces of the cruiser. So, anybody that wants to go home now can walk down the mountain to the nearest town and go home with full pay."

8 of my crew members decide to leave, I urge them to keep their mouths shut at least until we can go public with this whole scenario. "You have been part of a great adventure, let's keep it that way."

They walk off with all of us waving goodbye. Bob asks if we can stay here a few more hours as the power levels were mostly depleted during the submarine escape incident and it will probably take a few more hours in the sun to fully recharge the batteries. Not knowing just where to go at this time, so I agree. This will give me time to make plans. Where can we go and maintain the integrity of Bob and his crew members. I guess I've seen too many science fiction movies where aliens are captured and cut up to be examined by mad scientists. We can continue to hide out, but we still need to eat and that means we need to keep sneaking around at night or go public.

If I go to the military, just like the Navy, they will confiscate the spaceship and take all the advanced technology from it and turn it into military grade weaponry. I need to make a plan that will ensure the safety of Bob, his crew and all their technology they have aboard. We could always put this on the internet and have the world bid on the spaceship. How much would this bring? I thought, maybe 50 billion dollars. No, I'm not that kind of person, but so many people are. My crew, or what's left of them seem to have formed a friendship between all of us, an unspoken pact that we do whatever is necessary to protect each other and our new alien friends.

Chapter 28
HELLO AMERICA

It is getting well passed noon and the suns has been up in Japan for an hour or more. I flip open my lap-top and there it is, the sub. The Air Force Base in Misawa is swarmed with tens of thousands of locals since the news about the submarine got out. People flying drones and taking photos and the local police can't keep them back. International repercussions are happening. Apparently, there are no markings on the sub, and nobody has emerged from the sub yet. Speculation is running wild. It is time for me to make a phone call. I try and call the White House, but all lines are tied up. The Pentagon,

Joint Chiefs of Staff, newspapers, all jammed with people trying to claim responsibility of having knowledge of these incidents. I dial up my daughter.

Immediately she says, "What the hell have you been doing?"

I reply with. "Good to hear from you too."

I quickly explain to her what we did, briefly flip the camera around to show Bob and the rest of our combined crews in the command area.

I tell her "I need your help girl, I really do. Get yourself together and head down to Washington DC.

Try and get into the White House and President Potter. I need to speak to him personally, one on one with nobody interfering. It is much too important not to. The general population is going wild over this and it could hurt all the aliens, all five of them. I know its 3 hours away, but the White House is surrounded by thousands of people and it will probably get worse. So, I need you to work your way to the guards and tell them I left that calling card at the Misawa Air Force Base and get back to me. I must get the President to see for himself."

She agrees and hustles her way down to Washington DC with her lap-top and my message.

The traffic going into Washington DC is mobbed. Police have blocked off streets all around the White

House and there is not a single place to park. 20 blocks away in a residential area she finally finds parking place, but it is all of a mile and a half to the White House by foot. Lots of people crowded around all sides of the White House. She pushes her way to a guard house, there is nobody there to talk to, it is shut down and everybody is yelling they have some information too. She dials me up and tells me it's no use.

"None of the guards are talking to anybody, everybody is demanding access with some bull shit story."

I talk to her. "Please, do this for me and the rest of us. Go around the building, there will be an area sectioned off for the news crews. Find them, look for MSNBC or Fox News cameras and show them the pictures on your lap-top computer. I'll even send you a picture of the alien crew from the outside of the ship proving, we have the goods."

It's getting dark in Washington D.C., but she pushes and shoves her way thru the crowds to the far corner where she sees the news trucks and their antenna raised for satellite communications with each of their respective stations. It is roped off and a bunch of people are trying to get the attention of the camera crews. She pushes and pushes her way to the rope, ducking down and working her way between the front row and ducks under the rope. A guard comes over yelling for her to get back. She opens of her lap-top and with the picture I sent with myself and the aliens on the cargo ramp at the rear of the spaceship.

The guard sees the picture and immediately asks. "Is this real?".

"That's my dad, he is with them and needs to talk to President Potter, can you help me find the Fox News crew?"

"Sure lady," as he puts his hand on her back and points to the row of trailers and tells her. "Its three crews down, you can't see it now as it is behind the CNN crew. Good luck."

It's easy walking as the guard signals to another guard in front of her that it is alright for her to proceed.

She gets there and tries to get someone's attention as they are doing a live correspondent interview now with the White House as a backdrop. She cries out to them to look at her lap-top which she flips around showing the picture. One of the producers does, then holds up his hand and does the cut, wrap it up sign, waiving his hands vigorously over his head. The anchor notices the signals from the producer and quickly wraps up the interview with.

"It looks like we have some new information coming, will get back when we get this story."

The news anchor comes over, my daughter is totally flustered and tried to get some words out uttering.

"My dad, my dad needs to see the President, he is with the aliens now, look."

They look and see the pictures. They calm her down.

"My dad trusts Fox News to get the story right."

They started with asking her about the origins to get some sort of confirmation that she had first-hand knowledge. She pulls up an old email from me where I first contacted her. She shows them this is over 3 weeks old when my dad found the spaceship and shows the movie of the first underwater shots of the spacecraft.

"That's where my dad found it, got the Navy out there and then the Chinese sunk the ship and killed everybody else."

The news people were shocked. They haven't heard about the sinking of the cruiser, guess the government kept this quiet to keep us from going to war.

"See the pictures my dad sent me, the USS Port Royal is there just off the barge and it's gone now.

My dad said they even killed the crewmembers that go away. He was able to get into the spaceship with the aliens and could not be detected."

The news crew was astonished and speechless.

"My dad said the Chinese took the spaceship and strapped it to the sub, but the aliens were able to gain control of the sub and got it to the air force base in Japan. That's how the sub got there, that's all I know, but my dad needs to speak with the President."

"A Fox News Alert, just breaking news on the alien spaceship and the crew now on American soil somewhere on the west coast waiting to speak with the President of the United States. First contact and a Fox News exclusive report."

Well, that got the attention of all the crews around the White House and some officials inside the White House who were monitoring all the news channels. A White House staff member runs out to the Fox News crew area and asks where they got the information from.

"She is right over there being interviewed as we speak."

"Can you verify this?"

"We already have" said the news crew member.

"The President wants to see her right now," says the staffer.

Getting in to see the President isn't going to be easy, she has to go thru some quick identity and background checks, search for hidden object that might harm the president. Eventually she is brought to an office, not the oval office, were the White House Chief of Staff is waiting for her. He wants proof before he gets the President involved.

She dials me up again and says. "I'm in the White House now, where are you? They want to know where you are and can this be verified."

I reply. "I'm in the Olympic National Park behind Mount Olympus, that's the west side facing the Pacific Ocean. They can see the spaceship just off a fire trail and old logging trail just off Upper Hoh Road with a satellite shot or do a fly over with a military jet. We will waive to the pilot." I say in a jokingly manor. The Chief of Staff gets on the phone to the Air Force Command Center and they say they can divert a training flight of 2 F-15 fighter jets from a pursuit over the Pacific Ocean. They say a flyover will happen in about 15 minutes and when confirmed, the president will speak with me.

"Hurray for the red, white and blue." I shout in a half joking manor.

We go outside and wait for the visual fly over, in about 10 minutes 2 F-15 fighter jets from the local Air National Guard base fly over are due to fly over.

The 2 Air Force Reserve pilots were diverted from their training mission and told to observe and report back. They come in low, about 2,000 feet above the trees. On the first pas the lead pilot spots a silvery object half the way up the side of the mountain.

"That's got to be it" speaks the pilot. "It's got 2 massive engines in front and thrusters in the rear. It's some sort of flying object, but how did it get up here, no roads to speak of and nothing wide enough for that. There are a couple of Jokers waiving at us from the rear, is that what you wanted to know?"

"Affirmative" comes the reply.

We wave and the lead jet tips its wings in acknowledgement, they both put on the after burners and fly up and away banking towards the ocean and disappear into the high cloud partial cover as the sun starts to go down over the horizon. During this flyover I took out my super deluxe I-phone with its 30x telephoto lens and took a motion picture of the event and shared it with my daughter.

The Air Force calls back to the White House and confirms the fly over spotted a spaceship or something at the location provided. The chief of Staff required my daughter to stay put. They don't allow her to use the lap-top for personal use and someone stays in the room with her. It seems like an hour and it is starting to get dark out here with the twilight shimmering over the Pacific Ocean in the distance. I start thinking to myself, no wonder they call it America the beautiful. I get Bob out and show him the sun setting below the clouds and sunlight dancing off the water and the yellow glow of the bottom of the clouds and tell him "beautiful."

Chapter 29

MR. PRESIDENT

One of the crew members calls me and tells me. "We are back online, hurry up."

I run up the cargo ramp and all the way up to the command center and there on the screen is my daughter with a bright and wide smile covering her face and President Potter next to her.

"Good evening Mr. President" I say.

He replies with. "Your daughter tells me you go by Captain Rick."

"Yes sir Mr. President, captain of a mining barge that is." I think I'm losing my thoughts.

"Your daughter tells me you got the submarine onto the joint Misawa Air Force Base."

"Yes sir", I replied, "the Chinese sub sank the cruiser with 1 explosion and in 10 seconds it was gone.

They also killed all remaining members trying to escape. I personally witnessed that, and they thought they got us all when they sank the big plastic red escape boat. But we were able to hide inside the spaceship because of our new-found friends whom I have gotten to know and like. They are a peaceful race trying to find a new homeland from a dying planet. There is so much more I can tell you."

"Are you sure that they are Chinese? There are no markings on the submarine at the Air Force Base."

Asks the President.

"Yes. I am sure they are Chinese. They were on the deck of the barge and I could plainly see the markings and insignia on their uniforms."

"What do these aliens want?" the President asks. "How do you communicate with them?"

"Bob, that is who I call their commander and he was the first one to get revived. We spent a lot of time together learning the language and other fundamentals. He doesn't know it all. But he got enough from listening to conversations and watching TV shows while I slept. He is a quick learner as are all the remaining crew members. They offered to help us when we needed it the most and had no reserve thoughts about the Chinese sub incident. You could say that they could be a very strong ally for us to have. "

A long pause as the President ponders the situation at hand. "Well, why did you need to speak with me? Why don't you just meet with the generals at the Pentagon or where you at right now?"

I responded with "I've done that already and look what it got us, all-out war. Your Admirals were informed, they sent the cruiser to protect this asset, but couldn't. There are a lot of bad actor's out there who would do anything to get their hands on this technology. I need you to sanction their existence here, as the most powerful man in the world you could do just that."

The President ponders some more and asks; "What can I do."

I responded "You need to legalize their existence, make them American Citizens. That way they will be afforded all the rights others have and won't be taken to a secret experimental station and cut up into pieces in a place like Area 51. Maybe you could make a Presidential Proclamation or whatever you do to make them safe and secure here, so that no bad actors can steal from them or take what they have. To truly acknowledge their existence."

The President turns to my daughter and said. "your dad has a good point and a good heart. I'll get my legal department on it right away."

I thank the President and my daughter for all her effort.

"We are all getting hungry right now and will move to another location until we hear back from you.

Keep my daughter safe," I say.

Did we have a breakthrough or was it just political mumbo jumbo I heard. I don't know and I'm getting too tired to think of anything else. Well, we have another night to wait out the response from the President. After a nap, I wake up with the crew complaining that they are hungry. We have been here too long and need to move before somebody discovers us. I ask the crew if they have any ideas.

One of the young crew members, John, speak up. "My grandfather has a farm just outside Vancouver and it is not far from here, there is a good donut shop downtown."

Well, its nearby and not in America as the UFO hype is running ramped throughout the northwest states.

Chapter 30

OH CANADA!

The moon will not rise until after midnight so we can slip in undetected just above the treetops.

John's grandfather has a farm in Lulu just south of Vancouver that has been in the family for generations and residential areas have developed around it. We land a couple of hundred feet behind the old farmhouse in a well-established corn field. There seems to be a depression and one of the landing skids does not contact the ground properly. Bob tells the pilot to drag the spaceship about 50 feet closer to the farmhouse and spin around 180 degrees so then exit ramp faces the house and is parallel the corn rows by knocking down fully grown corn plants. After spinning the spaceship around we open the rear ramp. John and I leave the back of the spaceship and walk directly to the farmhouse in one of the furrows. John steps up onto the front porch, knocks on the front door and calls for his Grandpa. The door opens and John steps inside. A few minutes later he exits the house with the keys to his grandfather's car.

John is very excited to be driving into Vancouver. He tells me Lucky donuts are the best. As we get into downtown Vancouver, I see a pizza parlor. I tell John to stop, that pizza and sandwiches would be great as we have been eating donuts for days. We walk inside and I stare at the menus hanging from above the counter. I order 4 pizzas, one sausage, one pepperoni, one meat ball and 1 cheese pizza plus 4-foot-long sandwiches, 1 Italian, I meatball, 1 ham and cheese and 1 turkey. They ring up the order and

I pull out my wallet and hand him a handful of twenty dollar bills.

"We don't accept American money here." The counter person says. "Sorry."

John whips out his Canadian Western Bank Visa credit card, hands it to the counter person and said, "I never leave home without it."

Then I give John the money for his credit card and the donuts. It will, take 15 about minutes to prepare the order, so John leaves to get the donuts. I ask the counter person if I could take a couple of helium filled balloons left over from a kid's party earlier that day, he agreed. I need to charge my lap-top and the proprietor allows me to plug in as there is no plug-in port on the spaceship. As I watch out the window while the order is being prepared, I see Johns car coming back, but a Vancouver police car pulls him over just across the street from the pizzeria. The police officer gets John out of the car as the car was reported stolen by his grandfather. John hands the officer the registration and his license and shows him they both have the same last name.

"My Grandpa has Alzheimer's disease. He probably forgot he let me use his car. Call him."

The officer calls the station and gets the phone number on then complaint, puts it on speaker phone and asks the old man if he let his grandson use the car.

Grandpa responds with. "Jimmy, I forgot."

John yells, "Grandpa, Jimmy died over 10 years ago, I'm John, your other grandson."

"Oh, I know, little Johnny, but you are only 12 years old. I didn't give you the car to use, you are too young to drive."

John looked at the officer who understood exactly what he meant. He looked into the car and saw a bunch of hot drink cups, soda bottles and 4 boxes with a dozed donuts and bagels in them. He asks John what's going on with all that food.

John states. "I just flew in from Alaska and just had roller hockey a game with my old school pals."

The officer gives him back his papers and leaves. We get back to the farmhouse, John gives his grandfather back the keys and we walk back with our arms filled with food back to the spaceship through the corn field.

We take off and do like we did in Seattle and set down in the Garibaldi Provincial Park. Where everybody dives into the goodies we bought. I hand Bob a piece of cheese pizza.

He tries it and replied with. "Pissssah, good. Not as good as bagel and hot chocolate."

My remaining crew members start talking about their girlfriends and what they are going to do once they get home. Bob asks me about what they are talking about.

"What are girls, wives, bitches and hoooos?"

I explain that that we have 2 sexes, men do most of the hard labor work while the female members have children and raise them when they aren't working.

Bob looks at me pointing his finger into his chest saying. "Bob girl."

That never come up, and I had no idea. A bad assumption I made.

"I guess I have to start calling you Bobbie or Barbara, which do you prefer."

"Bob" she replies.

"Ok, its Bobby, not Bob."

Chapter 31
CIRCLES

Planes flying into and out of Vancouver International airport report a crop circle in a corn field just south of Vancouver easily seen from above being a number of straight lines with a semi-circle at one end. The local college sends out an investigation crew to grandpa's farm. They enter the farm with eco gear on and gigger counters sweeping the area. They see two sets of footprints going out from the road to the crop circle in one crop furrow and the footprints returning back to the road in an adjacent furrow.

They are standard boot prints, definitely not alien footprints. The amazing thing is that there is no footprints going from the edge of the crop figure to the other sections of the circle figures. No way they are connected so the prints may have been made by a local going into the field before the investigation crew got there.

I open my computer and get the local news and there is a buzz about aliens making a crop circle on John's grandfathers farm. We got busted again, but at least we didn't cause 15 accidents along a highway like we did in Seattle. This is crazy. We need to get something done. We can't keep hiding.

I'm sure everybody is anxious to get off this spaceship. A little later my daughter dials me up.

"Hi girl" I say as she swings the laptop around, "and Mr. President I see too."

The president introduces the Chief of Staff, Secretary of Defense, Secretary of Homeland Security and his National Science advisor, all standing behind him.

He looks at me and states: "Before we can go any further, we need to have some questions answered. My science advisor has some questions as well as the military staff that need to be clarified before we go any further and before we grant them anything."

The National Science advisor goes into a long statement. "As you know, and many people speculate that a rocket crashed near Roswell, New Mexico in 1947. A rocket about the size of a fighter plane was found crunched up into the side of a mountain. There were no aliens aboard, but we were able to recover some internal pieces which led to the electronic revolution. Inside there were a series of boards with microchips on them. Our scientists could not see the insides of them without a strong microscope.

The only thing they could make out was a series of switches. When we duplicated these very small micro bits, the best we could do was to make a singular switch that was the size of a standard nail head.

That was the first transistor and the world changed ever since. As we know, the evolution of electronics and super small chips evolved along the patterns found on this alien rocket. What did you have to do with this or what knowledge do you have about this incident?"

I look at Bobbie and we go into a huddle. President Potter and my daughter along with the staff members are watching us whispering to each other, pointing into the air and making hand gestures.

This goes on for about 10 minutes, then we break.

I start by saying: 'Bob, sorry, Bobby…. We first thought Bob was a male, but Bob is a girl, so it is now Bobby, and I tend to still call her Bob. Let me first state that Bob, I mean Bobbie and his, her, crew of 10 were the first to come to this planet about 100 million years ago. We can prove this as we have a full dinosaur skeleton on board. Let me show you."

I walk back to the crew quarters and turn my laptop to the bones still lying on the floor. They are amazed. I walk back to the command center as tell them.

"When Bobbie's ship launched from the other side of the galaxy, their sun was turning reddish and expanding. They knew it was just a matter of a few million years before the planet would be uninhabitable, so they sent out 2 spaceships, one to one side of the galaxy center core and the other went on the other side searching for places that they could migrate to. Bobbie has had no contact with the other ship as to where they went or what they found. Apparently, the other crews found something. Over the years they probably fully developed the planet that they were on and jumped to another and another moving closer and closer to earth. Bobbie seems to think that standard protocol is to send out unmanned probes to distant solar systems scouting for viable planets or moons to live on and these probes send back detailed information. There is some possibility that some manned spaceships reached here over 5,000 years ago when civilizations exploded onto the earth. Most of them with beliefs that gods from above gave them power to rule like the Egyptians, Greeks, Norse and Central American Indians all seem to point towards. That is a possibility, but we don't know for sure."

Bobbie didn't say all of this, I added lots of extra info into this. "But, we are here and their may be another faction that are looking at this planet. Bobbie seems to think they won't do anything as we have developed into our own civilization. It is not within their mandate to interrupt existing advanced life if it exists, only planets that have developed without intelligent beings."

The answer seems to suffice for the meantime. The Secretary of Defense has his question next.

"We didn't find anything explosive on board the spacecraft, but we did find a magnetic device that when we copied it we were able to produce the rail gun that uses magnetic and electrical impulses to sent a projectile out at a high rate of speed and is used as a weapon. What weapons do you have on board?"

Bobbie and I huddle again and discuss this briefly.

I respond with: "they do not have any offensive weapons at all. They have no wars and are not war like in nature as we are."

Bobbie shakes her head in agreement.

"The only weapon they have is like a Taser gun that can stun an attacker or kill it like the dinosaur you saw in the back of the spaceship. That's it" I say.

Homeland Security wants to know if the United States can use this to help defend us. Bobbie understands and we discuss this in a perplexing way. Perplexing because we are damned if we do and damned if we don't use this technology.

I respond with. "Making this technology available to 1 will mean others will steal, cheat and even kill for it as we just recently saw. Our new friends are willing to share some technology with the general commercial and industrial markets on a need to have basis. They will help keep peace among nations that threaten our existence as they want to become a part of the world at large. I must reiterate that these beings are not from a war like community, they are peace loving, gentle and caring as me and my crew have observed this past week, but I do realize 1 week does not predict a long-term pattern of actions. The rest is trust and trust is what we need to have from you. A trust that you won't take advantage of this situation and you will allow them to exist as separate people and respected them as such."

The President wants to finish up and recaps the events with the sinking of the cruiser. The Secretary of the Navy explains that the Navy underwater teams have been searching the area for the past week.

"The only part of the cruiser left intact is the hull from where the charges were placed to the bottom of the keel. There are 4 blast holes on each side and everything above is a mangled mess. The search teams are trying to recover bodies, but only a few of the 350 or more crew members were actually identifiable as human. The rest were just bone fragments and dog tags. The news about the sinking is being withheld from the public as the government is trying to recover the bodies and notify next of kin.

A great tragedy," he explains.

Now came the hard part, he wants to know who did this damned deed, did we have any proof it was the Chinese or was it the aliens. "No, no, we took pictures from inside the spaceship. The photos look a little distorted due to the difference in the vision range of the aliens, but you can plainly see the uniforms of about 30 or more military personnel running about the barge as I had explained to the President before. Did you capture any of the sub's crew members?"

I show the President and the staff standing behind the President some of my pictures taken from my cell phone and send them to my daughter's phone. I know they can't see the images in my hand but I keep talking as if they can point to the pictures and flipping from one to another. "Look, you can see one of the rocket engine trail smoke as it heads to the zodiac with the 2 guards aboard, see, the smoke trail didn't come from the barge or spaceship as it arcs too far away from us to have been fired from our location."

I do not know what else I can offer as proof that all we have said and been through is the truth. There is a long period with the President and the other staff members muttering in the background.

I chirp up again with. "Don't forget the submarine we put down in the middle of the air force base, we put it there and it is Chinese, right?"

They all agree after seeing the pictures we took from inside the spaceship of the Chinese military personnel that it was actually the Chinese submarine that sunk the USS Port Royal, not the aliens.

"We have to ask just 1 more question," said the President. "Did you or anybody aboard the spaceship actually see the submarine sink the cruiser?"

I ask everybody, including the aliens, if anybody actually saw the submarine sink the cruiser, they all shrug their solders, negatively nod their heads and say a unanimous no. The President stands up and tells us.

"I'll see what we can do to protect your friends."

The secretary of the Navy steps forward and adds. "Now that I have heard all the arguments and seen the evidence, I can state the following with confidence. The Bering Sea is not normally visited with Man of War capitol ships or submarines. We have listening buoys throughout the islands between Alaska and Russia. We heard nothing. Our readiness status was at DEFCOM 4, a low state of threat to our nation. I can only assume the captain of the USS Port Royal was under the assumption that there was no threat to his ship and anchored the vessel in place. This was a major mistake. Under normal operations the vessel would have kept in constant motion only slowing down to pick up and drop off security details for the barge."

"They might have even picked up the submarine if properly patrolling the waters off the coast and this incident could have been avoided. My sincere apologies to any inferences that you may have been made that any of you were involved in the sinking of our cruiser and the loss of the crew."

Chapter 32

BACK IN JAPAN

What do you do with a 600-foot-long super stealth submarine sitting in the middle of your runway?

Bang on the exterior hull and hope someone answers? The Air Force security personnel tried that, but nobody answers. The Chinese crew has strict orders from Beijing not to leave the submarine until they can figure out a diplomatic solution to the massive and embarrassing problem. The Japanese government along with the US Air Force Command are at odds over this. They debate to either take it off site or just lift it up and set it 100 feet off the runway. Regardless of what they decide, they start setting up a massive heavy lifting crane capable of listing 1,000 tons. It is so heavy it needs to be set up on a circular track to help support the weight. With all the clanging of metal during the assembly phase of the crane set up, the submarine crew pops up the periscope a few feet, undetected, just to see what was going on and they report back to Beijing.

The high command in Beijing has no answer for this, it wants to disavow itself of any wrongdoing like it never even happened. But how do they explain how a 2-billion-dollar prototype submarine just vanishes and ends up in the hands of the Japanese and Americans. There will be some heads rolling for this. Beijing gets back to the submarine captain. The order has come to set the warheads from the rockets and torpedoes throughout then sub and then set them all to explode at the same time for the total and complete destruction the sub and its secret electronics. The crew is gathered in their separate compartments as the captain gives the order to set the charges. The Chinese Army munitions specialists speaks up and asks the captain how much time should be allowed for the crew to surrender before the charges go off.

The captain replies. "There will be no surrendering."

As the forward section crew starts to set the charges, one member opens up the emergency escape hatch and sneaks out of the sub, then another member, then the rest of the forward compartment squad. The same thing happens in the rear of the sub until most of the crew has defected to the Japanese military police. Now with all the submariners that were working on setting the charges gone, the captain orders the officers to finish the job. They leave the sub too. That leaves just the captain and the loyal second in command. They just sit down and wait for the sub to be entered as the crew left all of the escape hatches open.

Chapter 33

CITIZENS AT LAST

At last, I get a call from the Joint Chiefs of Staff at the White House, it's all set up. Details to follow via email. I tell Bobbie that this will give them citizenship in America, the land of freedom and opportunity where I won't have to worry about their safety. Bobbie and the crew are excited. We wait for a few hours and then I get the email from an Air Force General at Andrews Air Force Base just outside Washington, DC. This Saturday coming up we will meet with President Potter. There is going to be a celebration with a military parade, the press and TV will also be present. They want us there about 2 hours before the proceedings start as not to startle the press and on-lookers.

They want our schedule so they can inform the radar stations, etc. I email them back we will be leaving the Cascade Mountains Friday night and fly along the Canada US border to the Great Lakes, follow them to Pennsylvania when we will drop straight down and follow the Potomac River where we will spend the remainder of the night in a state park near Harpers Ferry. Then, head south to Camp Springs, Maryland just off the I-95 Beltway, set it down at the Air and Space Expo Center at Andrews Air Force Base. I send the email and confirm that we will be there. Everybody is excited. I've got a 5 mile walk into town to get some supplies. I take a few of my men to help. We need food and supplies to last until Saturday.

It is very early Friday, predawn, and I'm getting antsy. My nerves are going haywire worrying something has got to go wrong somewhere. I get Willie and Sam to get the engines started and we are away to Washington, DC. I want to get to Harpers Ferry before daybreak as not to be seen and cause a commotion. One of the things gnawing away at me is there is no news about the upcoming event. The invitation stated the press and TV stations would be present, so should they not be announcing this upcoming event?

Skimming over the great lakes at over 2,000 miles per hour I become cynical, my other natural state. I ask the science officer, Pete, if they have high resolution telescopes.

Pete replies. "We can see halfway across the galaxy if needed."

I talk with Bobbie about my fears and she seems to think it is wise to be precautious in nature. I want to go up, way up, 50+ miles so we won't be seen by aircraft and local radar. Then hover over the meeting place, so I want to be 1/2 to 5/8 of the way up to the edge of space. Bobbie understands and orders her crew to quickly zip up to a high post and hover. Bobbie lets me know that hovering in place is much harder than running along magnetic lines of flux. Flux lines can change violently when the solar winds interrupt the earth's magnetic lines causing the flux lines to bend and move around, but we do it as the sun is in a quiet period of only a few sun spots.

Looking down in the predawn hours I see military transport trailers bringing in Abrams M-1A tanks and being off-loading behind the hangers. We hoover all day and watch the base for additional activity, nothing but airplanes being moved out of the hanger closest to the Air and Space Expo Center. I wonder if I was just being overly nervous about this upcoming ceremony. Maybe they just brought the tanks in for a military operation. Maybe they moved out the planes as a show of our flying capabilities, or maybe they are going to take the spaceship and put it into the hanger.

Saturday pre-dawn 9 buses pull into the and circle around behind one of the larger hangers. It looks like 40 or more troops off load from each bus and directly behind them are support trucks which off load

Guns and rocket launchers which we can plainly see from above with the high-resolution imaging. There has been no setting up of a reception area and press area that one would expect for this kind of reception. Again, listening to local and national news channels, no word of this event. CNN is reporting that the President is meeting with a trade delegation from South America around the same time we are to meet. Something definitely rotten is going on here. Is this really going to happen. The time approaches when we are supposed to arrive and the area surrounding is buzzing with military aircraft, part of the welcome mat I presume, but what kind of a welcome. No press, no TV set up. I check up on the Presidents location again and no external activity. I have the telescope turn to the White House and no Marine 1 helicopter on the lawn which is standard procedure if he is going to Andrews Air Force Base. Marine 1, 2 and 3 are still parked at Andrews Air Force Base.

I turn to Bobbie and say, "we have been betrayed, I don't think the President knows about this, he has been kept out of the loop so the military can get this technology. We need to do something else decisively and do it right now."

We can't hide forever. There are numerous other countries that we can go to, but the President is the leader of the free world. If we go to a small free country, they won't be able to provide the protection from bad actors like China tried to do to us. We need to crash in on the President of the United States of America. Land on the south lawn and hope for the best. What could possibly go wrong? Or even more haunting within my brain, what could possibly go right? I take a minute with Bobbie and her crew, I try to explain my thoughts as to how to proceed. Bobbie huddles with her crew members, turns around after a somewhat lengthy conversation and says.

"What you think good for us, we do it. We trust you."

Going up in a fast-moving elevator isn't too bad, but coming down is always a bad feeling. Especially when you stop and your stomach reaches your knees. I give Bobbie the order and here we gooooooo.

Pinned to the seat for 50 miles straight down holding my breath as long as I can, and oh, the stopping.

Bobbie and the alien crew laugh at us. It doesn't affect them like it does us. We stop about 100 feet above the south lawn of the White House which allows anybody out there to clear a spot while we slowly decent to the ground. We stirred up the hornet's nest as many of the secret service and guards with dogs immediately surround us.

The secret service in the White House grabs the President and starts to maneuver him to the elevator going to the underground situation room, but as he is being pushed past a window, he spies the spaceship and tells the guards.

"Stop, STOP." He orders as that is the spaceship he has been seeing over the past week, "I've got this, we have been talking, what made them come here, now?"

I tell Bobbie to slowly open the rear hatch which is facing the White House. I go all the way to the back and slowly walk down the ramp with my hands up and my laptop in my left hand. I am immediately surrounded by men and women with guns pointed at me and dogs barking. I stand there for what seems like hours or an eternity until President comes out with a few secret service personnel.

"Make a hole for the President." Orders are being shouted.

" You must be captain Rick?" The President says.

"Yes, Yes, I am" I reply. "And I have some very interesting people for you to meet. Alien people that is."

The President inquires, asking me as to why we came to the White House so expectantly. I slowly open up my lap-top and flip to the letter.

"I received this letter just 4 days ago inviting me to meet you at Andrews Air Force Base."

President Potter responds by saying "I didn't schedule any meeting. Nobody spoke of this to me.

Who was to meet you there?"

I show him the letter from the Joint Chiefs of Staff and is explicitly states that the President will be there to meet you. It was on the right letterhead and had the correct signatures. President Potter tells all the guards and secret service members to back off. He turns to call his staff, but it seems that all the staff members and all the White House employees are hanging out windows or line up on the patio 4 deep just to see what's going on with a spaceship in their back yard.

He yells to his staff. "Get the Joint Chiefs here right now."

Then asks me if he can see the aliens in person. I repeated from our last conversation.

"They have no weapons. I just have a pistol which I grabbed when the Chinese attacked for protection from the unknown, I'll give it to the guards. So now, it wouldn't be appropriate to have your guards point their guns at visiting dignitaries would it?"

The President agrees and orders all guards to secure their weapons and stand back. Bobbie and all the others are waiting at the top of the ramp. President Potter can see their legs partially in the light inside the spaceship, so he waves for them to come out. I do, likewise, calling them out and waving my arms too.

Bobbie calls the crew to attention, they line up and smartly march down the ramp, make a 90 degree turn to the left and line up in front of the President, stop, smartly do a right face and all together pound their chest with their right hands, then extend arm out with palms up and then do a salute with their hands to the forehead and smartly down to their sides.

"I'm impressed." The President says.

He and walks forward with his hand out to greet each one. I stand behind them and call out each name we gave the crew as they shook the President's hand. Bobbie, Willie, Sam, Pete, and George, and lastly, the President shook my hand and invited us all to come in for something to drink. The President asked me as to what they might like to have.

All in unison, the answer came back. "Hot chocolate and butter bagel."

I yell. "Don't let anybody near that machine."

And the security guards surround the spaceship.

President Potter takes on the short tour of the White House while the cooks prepare the hot chocolate and bagels as requested. We all sit down at this very long table with Bobbie and her crew on one side and myself and my crew on the other side with the President in the middle on the end so we all can see one another and converse. The President wants to know more about the meeting and why we didn't go there. I flip open my lap-top and show him pictures I took while inside the ship of the display board within the spaceship showing the military activity, Marine 1, 2 and 3 all setting on their landing pads, the tanks and soldiers that had positioning themselves.

"It looked like a trap to me Mr. President, a forceful military take-over of the spaceship and control of those inside." I reply.

Then the bagels and hot chocolate arrived. It was like a children's birthday party as the crews broke the bagels in half and dipped them into the hot chocolate over and over. The president looked to me and inquired just as to why they were so excited.

"I guess they just didn't have that kind of food where they came from. Chocolate is the most favorite flavor here, now it seems to be the most favorite flavor in the entire galaxy." I state.

The President leans over to me and asks if they always eat like this.

I tell him. "Just wait until they try double deep chocolate fudge cake and banana split ice cream."

While we were having our bagels, 2 separate convoys of vehicles pull up to the White House, the first Convoy of vehicles contains the Speaker and minority leaders of the Senate and the House plus ranking members of the Armed Forces Committee and the Intelligence Committee. Just a few minutes' behind than the Joint Chiefs of Staff and their attaches arrived. They were all standing in the grand foyer wondering why they were summoned. The President told his chief of staff to bring them in. They filtered in and seeing the aliens in the White house started mumbling to themselves. Some went behind Bobbie and his men, some behind me and my crew.

President Potter stands up but gives us the stay seated hand signal.

"Meet our new-found friends from the other side of the galaxy. I'm sorry I didn't have sufficient time to make a proper reception for our guests, and guests they are. Our military Chiefs of Staff decided that they would meet them without our knowledge and disgrace us and our beliefs of freedom for all peoples. I want all of your resignations on my desk within the hour and now I want to know why I shouldn't strip them of all rank and give them a dishonorable discharge immediately."

The Admiral steps forward and states. "It was me Mr. President, myself and the Secretary of the Navy. After what happened to the USS Port Royal loosing 350 souls, we decided to get with the other generals and keep the possibility of this happening here. Keeping it all under wraps and putting the spaceship in a hanger out of sight so we could study it. Everybody agreed, we were just trying to protect you, Sir."

The members of congress start talking amongst themselves.

The President interjects. "Did any of you in congress know about this planned military coup, anybody?"

Nobody speaks up, they all lower their heads and shake them in a negative response.

The President speaks up. "These visitors want to become American citizens. They may be the last of their kind anywhere in the galaxy as far as they know and what will it take, an act of Congress to make them a lawful citizen of America. We, I do mean all of us, must do something to protect them from the curiosity seekers and fortune hunters and other bad actors that would take without asking. I have had some of the legal staff members look into this, and the best that they have come up with is the aliens were found off the Alaskan coast in our protected waters just a mile or more offshore which makes the Alaskan residents, but they were not born here, and they would be considered illegal aliens, no pun intended. But they were here before Alaska was purchased and before the first people settled in the new world so that makes them the original inhabitants of Alaska, therefore they can be considered as a natural Indian tribe and given the protected status of such. Do you all agree?"

They all answer in the affirmative.

"So, pass a resolution in the House, get it thru the Senate and onto my desk by the end of the week, or maybe sooner if you think you have it in you."

During this time as the press corps was gathering, some that were outside the White House covering the South American trade delegation saw the spaceship land and 1 crew got tape of it landing, but couldn't see much other than the top of the spaceship after it landed from their prospective. Cameras rolling and TV anchors giving their take on this magnificent spaceship and tying it into the sightings along the northwest coast a week ago, making all sorts of speculative comments while waiting for the President to appear.

We walk towards the door to the south lawn with President Potter in the lead. Just as we get to the door, he invites Bobbie to be at his right-hand side. Then he turns around and points to me to come up to his left side. Me, Me I think to myself in my blue jean work clothes while Bobbie is in his uniform that never seems to get dirty or even a wrinkle. Me I think again, what a lollipop. As we walk out the door, cameras flashing, news correspondents from all over the world shouting questions wanting to be the first ones to ask the President a question. The President reaches the podium while we stand behind him. Holds his hands up and greats the American public.

Then says those magic words. "We are not alone in this universe; we have visitors who have come to me and requested asylum. Those rumors you heard about in the Northwest, Alaska and northern Japan are true. There were battles fought and perils overcome to get here, we lost one of our front-line cruisers to a covert operation by the rouge Chinese Navy commanders, but they are hear and safe now and I officially grant them temporary citizenship until such time that we can figure out their names, birth date and place of origin."

Questions fly at the President, but most are deflected to a future date when Bobbie and her crew can be properly questioned by professionals in various fields. The President bends over and to his right and asks Bobbie if she can have a tour of the spaceship. Bobbie claps her hands in excitement and agreed.

Bobbie tells her crew to wait while Bobbie, myself and the President inspect the inside of the spaceship. The secret service members want to accompany then President, but he shakes them off.

I tell them. "We aren't going anywhere without the pilots, and they are standing over there. I have been with these amazing friends for almost a month now. They have shown no hostility towards me and the crew, only gratitude. They calmly assisted in our escape from the submarine in a professional manor. They even rejoiced at our success. We have bonded as a team and respect one another. I have every confidence that they are peaceful and will not be a threat to anyone."

President Potter was amazed at all the equipment and building materials, but not 1 tank or war like robots with red eyes shooting laser beams was to be found. When we enter the crew's quarters and stasis room, the dinosaur bones and leathery skin that have been glued to the floor with the rotted liquified flesh turning to a sticky paste like substance. The President was taken aback by the stark reality that dinosaurs were real and deadly. He sees the crew stasis pods where the crew members were just lying in place for eons. On into the control cabin where you can see out of the translucent metallic windows in the front. Even though they have a reddish tint to them, he could plainly see the massive crowds developing along the south gates. He asks me why the red lighting. I explain that their sun, star was older than ours and was growing larger and turning red. That is why they had to leave as their sun was coming to its end of its life span.

"Mr. President, Sir, what these travelers need is a permanent home, a place that they won't be pestered by sightseeing Space Trekkies. Somewhere, where the climate is warm and the elevation is below 1,000 feet. Maybe a semi deserted island in the Hawaiian Islands like Kahoolawe, minimally populated and restricted access. They have so much to offer with their technology. They can be of assistance to the Space Force by shuttling materials back and forth to the moon without rockets, patent technology for innovations in farming, industry and general health. But they need you to get the ball rolling, Sir."

Chapter 34
Q AND A

After the meeting with President Potter and the proclamation giving citizenship to the aliens. I guess I have become the center of all requests and the agent for the crew. Requests from all over the world have been pouring in. Some offering up to a million US dollars in appearance fees. We sit down and have a long chat, Bobbie and the rest of the crew can now speak well, but still don't know all the words and meanings attached in sentences. We, as a group decide that first appearance should be to the scientific community. It's only fair to let the worlds smartest minds have the privilege of asking sensible questions as the world does have the right to know more about these aliens, but to get the stories right and accurate. Invitations come in from all over, MIT, Princeton, Yale, Harvard, Maryland, USC, Stamford, Japan, England and so forth. We settle on Princeton University as it is located halfway between MIT and the Beltway around Washington DC and easy access off U.S. Highway 1.

In conjunction with Princeton University and their staff we agree that 10,000 tickets will be sold at $1,000 a seat and only with credentials of know accomplished scientists and to some of the world's top minds. Within 24 hours we get over 25,000 applications complete with resumes and full deposits for the seats. We close the applications and agree that the top 5,000 will be accepted and the rest drawn by lottery with each application being assigned a number. This takes days, but within the week the arena is being set up for the following Saturday.

The big day finally arrives, the center is filled with anticipation. Most everybody that enters asks if they can ask a question at which we respond that 20 experts in many fields have been selected and will be allowed to ask 1 question at a time. Physics, math, theology, medicine, and other related fields were chosen to ask.

"Write down your question and it will be reviewed by our staff when time allows, they will each be reviewed and answered on merit."

The large TV screens throughout the center are showing pictures of the journey we all took getting here. My first underwater pictures of the space craft, pictures on the barge, pictures of the Chinese insurgency, pictures of the submarine in Japan, pictures of the crop circle, outside the Dunkin Donuts shop in Seattle from planes flying over with their I-phones, pictures with the president and many more.

Groups stand sometimes 20 deep looking at the photos before entering the seating areas. And still the big TV boards show more photos and movies of the aliens. There is a circus like atmosphere going on here.

We, me and all the alien crew members, walk in once most of the visitors are settled. They all stand up and applaud. The introductions are made. I, captain Rick, get to introduce the crew.

I state that "I named the commander of the mission Bob. Another crew member of mine was a Hermit's fan and named the pilot and co-pilot Willie and Sam from one of their songs. Of course, that crew members name is Henry and he keeps on singing I'm Henry the VIII I am over and over. It kind of gets stuck in your mind. The science officer is Pete, and finally the engineer George."

We all sit down after a brief round of applause. Bob looks at me and smacks me on the back of my head.

I respond with, "I forgot, we named them all for male names assuming they were all males, but 3 of them are females, Bobbie, Willie and Samantha. We still call them by their original names, but Bob is too much a masculine name so we now call her Bobbie."

We settle down and the 1st question comes.

"We hear that you have super-human strength, jump 10 feet at a time, can you elaborate on that."

"Certainly" I respond. "one of my crew members must have spoken to the press. Yes, they can jump 10 feet into the air as one or more have done while we were on the ground just to exercise all their muscles being cooped up for so long. But super-human is not quite right. When we go to the moon we can certainly jump for great distances with ease, likewise, their original planet was larger than ours and had a greater gravitational force, so this is easy for them to jump 10 feet, but they can't pick up a bus and toss it across the street like in the movies. Nothing like that."

Bobbie responds with "Our planet has 1.4 times the gravity of earth and a larger diameter than earth."

I interrupt with. "1.4 your number system or 1.4 times our number system. There is a difference."

"1.4 our numerical system." Replies Bobbie.

Next question comes. "How does your numerical system relate to our physics and math?"

Bobbie responds with "It is difficult for us to understand your numbers, we learned from the time we were little children. Our system is easy for us, we think our system, and we work our numbers the same way you do with formulas, but numbers are different to you, but have same meaning to us. An example is that it is a lot faster for me to count from 1 to 101 in my system than in your number system. I only need to use 65 numbers to get to my 101 while you need 101. But the number 101 is different to us that to you. Our computers see them as your 65, but we know what it means in our number system."

Next question. "How have you been able to adapt to our planet and why did you leave your planet?"

"That's 2 questions, but since they are related, we will try and answer them as best we can." Bobbie speaks up. Captain Rick makes funny at us much of time. When he sees a helium balloon, he sucks it in and speaks in a high squeak voice at us and we all laugh. Just the same, your air has more helium than our planet had, and our voice is squeaky to you."

I cut in with "there is also an altitude problem, when we were parked in the mountains they had a hard time breathing as their planet had a much denser atmosphere than ours so they didn't go outside much when up at a higher altitude except to see the beautiful sunsets."

Bobbie buts in with; "Your star is yellow and has developed over millions of years. Our planet is."

I interrupt with "our years or your years?" the crowd laughs.

"Your years, mine years, still a long time." Bobbie responds. "Our planet is farther from star than yours and took longer to grow up. When our star yellow, our planet too cold to develop other than small cell life, but it made an atmosphere. Our star turn orange and got big, big enough to warm it up so life can grow. As we, (a pause)."

I interrupt once again with the word "Develop."

"Develop," Bobbie continues. "Star still changing to red and get bigger. We know we need to find another home we can live on; we all will die soon." Mumbling throughout the audience.

Another question comes in. "Do you believe in God?"

I reply "That is the 500-pound gorilla in the room and that is not an appropriate question for this venue."

Bobbie smacks me on the back of the head again and says. "Not for you, I answer." The crowd chuckles. "We believe we are all one people and one planet. We cannot live without our planet, we take care of planet, planet take care of us, we re…spect it as our own mother."

A question is floored that many scientists have been waiting for, "How fast does your space craft travel? Can you go faster than the speed of light?"

Bobbie replies "we go half max speed easy, faster when not too much push back, not max speed, 5/8 maybe 6/8 max speed."

I whisper a conversation with Bobbie, then I continue with; "They cannot attain the speed of light as the spacecraft has too much resistance against the dark matter in space. Maximum speed depends upon how dense the matter is, and deep space has many areas of differing density. I guess the main problem is in order to obtain enough material for enhanced propulsion the profile of the spacecraft needs to be larger making resistance higher and it becomes a proportional problem of power verses resistance."

Next question comes in as. "Are you going to share your technology with us?"

"NO" I reply quickly, "no."

Bobby smacks me again, "Yes."

I say "No" again and smack my hand on the deck, "No."

Bobbie smacks her hand on the table deck and says "Yes, but not now, later."

I reply again with "I need to qualify that answer. We area very young species while Bobbie's is from a much more mature species. We have been warring throughout history and still are. Bobbie and her crew would like nothing better than to share their technology with us to make our world a better place.

They have technology that can clean up our atmosphere and stop global warming, but they also have technology that can be used by us against one another. We have decided to release some technology that won't hurt our current lifestyle or endanger or empower one people over another. But, for the rest, that is for you, as a single community of people, you need to show that you are responsible enough to handle these gifts."

Bobbie puts her hand over my mouth. "I speak now, not you. You have 1 moon, we had 2. One round like your moon, and another" Bobby stretched out her arms, "long, not so big and closer to the planet than the big moon. When our people got new techno…ology, all people can do what they want.

They can go to moon and mine like you drive to work. Our Mr. President's sold mining rights to people from all over. For hundreds of years our people mined this moon, made holes in and out, make many of our people rich, more and more go to mine the moon. One day as moon structure becomes week, the star, planets and moons all in one line. Star, big planets, my planet, small moon, big moon, biggest planet and our moon pulls apart, then they fall down to planet, big rocks hit many cities, kill everybody.

Small rocks hit and many, many of my people die."

Bobby writes down a series of numbers hundreds, thousands, millions, to billions. "Billions die and we change. No more money, every people work the job they have, get food, rooms for living, all things we need. That starts the new era, we do not look back, we learn."

Another question. "I understand that you have in your possession, intact, a complete set of dinosaurbones. Are we as able to examine these bones?"

I put my hand on Bobbie shoulder and speak. "We are talking with the Field Museum in Chicago at this time. They have one of the most extensive paleontology departments anywhere. As you may have heard, there is no degradation of the bones as they have not been buried and fossilized over the millions of years. This is a complete set of bones, naturally white with all calcium and inner structures intact.

Our main problem is the DNA that might remain. We are afraid that scientist everywhere will rush to recover full or partial strands of the DNA and revive the raptor as a living artifact. You must remember that the smartest people can do the stupidest things. Reviving an extinct species of one of the most intelligent and feared raptors ever with no natural enemies that kept their numbers down. There is no current natural counterbalances out there today. One pregnant raptor getting loose can produce tens of thousands of offspring over a ten-year period, and you'll never find them. What you may not know is that half of the crew was killed by a single pack of raptors. That is 6 members of the commander's crew that was revived, and they only killed 1 raptor, and that was probably an accident. Imagine a thousand raptors living in the deep swamp in the Everglades. Eventually they will consume all the alligators, snakes, manatees, and other indigenous animals. The only thing they will have left is us. Your worst nightmare will come true. We are working out a deal where all the bones, teeth and skin left will irradiated to destroy all the DNA that might remain as the spaceship has a cleansing system that removed all bacteria and viruses that might have been in the air as the bodies rotted within. So, the answer is. The bones will be available for paleontologists to examine for a period to be determined before being put on display to the public. Another item that Bobbie and the rest of the crew have all agreed that the bones of the killed crew member which are also intact will be available for study. This may bring you to another question, the entire crew has already spent days being examined by medical staff with a complete make up of x-rays, echoes, cat scans, blood work, etc. The results will.be available on-line soon."

"We have a hand-written question submitted by the NASA Jet Propulsion Laboratory. It reads."

"You, our alien friends, have no visible propulsion systems while cruising around this planet. How are you able to obtain velocity, trajectory and altitude without engines?"

Bobbie asks Pete to answer. "Pete is our science officer and will answer this question for the audience. He may not be able to give you all the answers you want. But here is Pete."

"You already have started on the path towards the answer. I have been researching some of the mechanical advances you as a people have made. One such innovation is the beginning to understanding how our inner solar system propulsion works. Magnetic Levitation, or as you call it Maglev. You have been working on this system for over 50 years and can move a 100-ton train over 300 miles per hour along without touching anything. Completely suspended above the rails with magnets.

That is somewhat like the way we got started and it took hundreds of our years to get to the magna flux engines we use. The Maglev system uses a rail as the medium to lift the weight of the train up and off the rails. Our system turns this inside out and uses the magnetic field as the medium to hold up the spacecraft. Unlike a fixed rail, we can concentrate the magnetic force lines in such a way to give propulsion and direction to the spacecraft. We will be…."

Pete stretches around Bobbie and whispers in my ear for the right word to use. I give it to him.

"Patent was the word I was looking for, patenting our innovations in such a manor as it can be of use to all peoples. But we will do it over a period of time when you, as an entire people, are ready for it.

We have been answering questions for over 5 hours now and, I don't know about you, but I am exhausted. All this has been transcribed and a full copy will be sent to you when it is completed.

Thank you all for your enthusiasm.

Chapter 35

WHAT IS NEXT

Now that the Federal Government has granted our visitors full citizenship, protected Native American Citizen status and an island with limited access, here is what Bobbie and his crew have agreed to do:

1. Share technology with NASA for their ion propulsion engines.

2. Form a corporation for alien technology and the use thereof which will include:

3. Weekly 30-hour tours to the moon including a moon walk

4. Once every 1 ½ years when Mars is closest to earth have a 2-week excursion to the planet including 1

full day on the surface.

5. Use the spaceship to haul materials for the U.S. Space Force Command for the construction of off earth facilities as the spaceship can haul as much materials and personnel as 20+ separate rocket launches in 1 day as compared to months or even a year for conventional rocket transportation.

Of course, they will charge fair fees for their services which will be used for the protection of our new planet's environment, security of their homeland and securing a future for their peoples now and in the future. We will think of more.

Chapter 36
BOBBIE'S WORLD

It's now winter and I get an invitation from Bobbie to visit their new settlement they have been building for the past few months on an old abandoned naval artillery and bombing range on then island of Kahoolawe after the Hawaiian government deeded the property to them along with the Island Commission's approval. I landed on Maui, then chartered a helicopter flight to Kahoolawe and the new Settlement for Bobbie and the crew. They were all so proud of what they had accomplished is a short time by building living quarters, water and waste treatment facilities and having cleared over 1 square mile of unexploded bombing ordinance and removing metal fragments from the soil. They brought me over to see their big machine they used for clearing bomb fragments, vegetation and leveling the land.

It looked like a bulldozer, but much larger, like a D-20.

I asked Bobbie; "Where did you store that monster" as it was too big to fit in the spaceship.

Bobbie replies "many boxes all over the cargo area, some assembly required."

That got a laugh.

We went over to their living quarters, the headroom was a little low for me, but I managed to keep from bumping my head. We sat down and started chatting and catching up on where we had been and where we were looking to go to, small talk, nothing important.

After a while I asked Bobbie; "You didn't ask me to come all the way out here just for small talk, what's up?" Bobbie looked away for a moment and tears swelled up in those big black eyes and I could see she was having trouble getting out the words.

Then Bobbie began with; "I have not told you much about our world, it has been heavy on our hearts, but we didn't know the technological words to explain many things and we didn't know if you were ready for us. Now that we have this place to live, I can freely tell you about our home world."

I put my hand up and stop Bobbie, reach into my carry bag and got a camera recorder and set it up knowing this may be of some importance. Then I signal Bobbie to continue by waiving my hand towards me as the recording started. Bobbie resumed.

"I have been studying the history of this planet and your scientist's rendition of how it was formed, how life started and the evolution of life got to the present day. It is somewhat flawed, but adequate as your people are still filling in the missing pieces. But this conversation is not about your world, it is about ours, or what our world was like if it even still exists. Our star is, or was, slightly larger than yours, maybe 10% larger, maybe more. Our planet was formed in a similar manor as yours. But it is 40% larger and has over 50% more gravity than this planet. Our solar system consisted of 7 planets, 2 of which were inside our orbit and being much larger gas giants. Why do you call them giants when only your larger people are giants? That doesn't seem right to me as we call them protectors. The protectors have many moons as they are the trash collectors of our solar system. We had our two moons and another protector beyond our orbit with the remaining 3 being much smaller, like your Mars. We called them protectors as they could catch or absorb dangerous space debris from hitting our planet. We believe out smaller inside moon, the one that broke apart was placed there by one of the protectors after it tried to pull in an asteroid and couldn't keep it, but slowed it down enough to fling it into an orbit between our home world and the moon. The rest is history as you might say."

Bobbie continues. "Getting back to our world. It is located somewhere beyond where your Mars is located at the far edge of the life zone, too cold for life to form except for small one celled life forms and some small higher functioning life which formed around the thermally heated areas when we still had active tectonic plates. But as the planet cooled, the crust got too thick for the kind of movement your planet experiences. These organisms produced oxygen from the sulfuric and carbon compounds in our atmosphere. We had water, but less than half of the amount you have here. Our star had the same make-up as this star, but when it got to be the age of your yellow star there was no advanced life on our planet. It took another 2 billion of your years, less than 1 billion of our years for our star to start to turn orange and reddish and expand to about double the size of this star. When this happened, our planet was now in the warm life-giving zone that you enjoy. Life flourished, but it did not develop the same as yours. Maybe too much infra-red light, maybe too much gravity, but the mammalian species developed quickly without those horrible lizards, dinosaurs and such that this world had to start with. As our ownspecies was developing, the star was getting older, but still life giving. Our civilization flourished to what it was when I left the planet. When I left our home world, we had more oxygen in the atmosphere and less helium, more hydrogen as it wasn't as easy for it to escape our gravity and maybe that is why our voices are altered and we cannot sustain higher altitudes where the oxygen is thinner."

Bobby clears her throat.

"Once again I am off the path that I want to go in. I am the oldest member of the crew by far. Our lifespan was about 350 of your earth years on our home planet, our reproductive rate is very slow. I have been on many missions where my body was put into stasis and that takes its toll by reducing the life expectancy by many of our years. We do not know how the effects of this planet will change our lives, our lifespan and our ability to reproduce, but the good news is that we will be having a new addition within the next year. Unfortunately, our resident doctor tells me I am reaching the end of my life cycle, too soon, but I do not know when. Maybe before the new child arrives, maybe not. But we all have agreed to call him Captain Rick in your honor."

Tears come to my eyes as this surreal news sinks in. I tell them. "That is the cycle of life we earthlings know and accept. I will miss you, Bobbie, but drop the Captain from that name." I stop the recording and walk out for a breath of fresh air. Sam opens the door and re-invites me back in.

"We have a special treat for you, our new favorite dinner."

We step back into the structure and all sit down at the dinner table, well, they do. I don't seem to fit into a child size chair and table, so I sit down in a squat position on the floor at the end of the table.

Both Willie and Sam bring in big bowls, big for them, topped off by what looks like whipped cream.

Willie hands me my bowl and says "Rocky Road ice cream with hot fudge and whipped cream, our favorite."

I respond with "that's not diner, that's dessert."

Bobbie interjects, "We don't like our food anymore, your food is so good to our tastes that every meal is a celebration. But this is our favorite and why wait until after diner to have what we want the most?"

I get invited to spend the night and rehash our experiences over again, but their beds are so small and I won't be able to fit, so I respectfully decline, but tell them next time I'll bring my own bed with me.

I give them all a hug as if they were my children, say my goodbyes and board the waiting helicopter. Iknow in my heart that I may never see Bobbie again. What an adventure this has been.

THE ADVENTURE CONTINUES

www.ingramcontent.com/pod-product-compliance
Lightning Source LLC
LaVergne TN
LVHW011949070526
838202LV00054B/4868